The
CHOCOLATE
Shark Shenanigans

The
CHOCOLATE
Shark
Shenanigans

A CHOCOHOLIC MYSTERY

JoANNA CARL

BERKLEY PRIME CRIME
NEW YORK

BERKLEY PRIME CRIME
Published by Berkley
An imprint of Penguin Random House LLC
penguinrandomhouse.com

Library of Congress Cataloging-in-Publication Data
Names: Carl, JoAnna, author.
Title: The chocolate shark shenanigans / JoAnna Carl.
Description: First edition. | New York : Berkley Prime Crime, 2019. |
Series: A chocoholic mystery
Identifiers: LCCN 2019006881| ISBN 9780593100004 (hardcover) |
ISBN 9780440000259 (ebook)
Subjects: | GSAFD: Mystery fiction.
Classification: LCC PS3569.A51977 C498 2019 | DDC 813/.54—dc23
LC record available at https://lccn.loc.gov/2019006881

First Edition: November 2019

Printed in Canada
1 3 5 7 9 10 8 6 4 2

Cover art by Ben Perini

TO TRACY PAQUIN AND SUSAN McDERMOTT

Friends and Neighbors

Acknowledgments

It takes a village to write a book, or at least it takes me one. Friends and relatives who helped with this book include: Jim Avance, experienced lawman; Dr. Rosemary Bellino, a wise and friendly doctor; Betsy Peters, daughter and former chocolatier; Elizabeth Garber, proprietor of Best Chocolate in Town, Indianapolis; Joan Houghton, banker and friend; Frank Conklin and John Naberhaus, both Realtors; Josh Henderson, engineer and general fun guy; and Kim Kimbrell, architect.

In addition, two arts supporters from Lawton, Oklahoma, presented generous gifts to the Lawton Arts for All campaign in exchange for the right to have their names used in this book. Many thanks to Twyla McDonald and James "Sharpy" Brock.

The
CHOCOLATE
Shark Shenanigans

Chapter 1

Never hire a nosy plumber.

They ask questions all the time. This means you don't have a chance to ask questions yourself. Important questions, such as "Why is it leaking?" or "Does it need to be replaced?"

Instead, you're answering the plumber's questions. Meaningless questions, such as, "Wasn't the family who lived in this house mixed up in some crime, way back sometime?"

A nosy plumber will drive you crazy. I was convinced of this as "Digger" Brown tapped on pipes in the basement ceiling of the Bailey house.

The Bailey house represented a new business enterprise for my husband, Joe Woodyard, and my uncle, Hogan Jones. Flipping. Not hamburgers. The house.

Joe and Hogan wanted to buy a house—one that happened to be near the one Joe and I lived in—remodel and update it, then sell it at a profit. I wasn't enthusiastic about the project, but I had been assigned a job anyway. I was showing the potential plumber around so he could give us an estimate.

Digger was Joe and Hogan's first choice of plumber. I

couldn't figure out if they favored his work because the guy was a top-notch plumber or if they liked him because of friendliness for his father, whose business Digger had taken over after an older son failed to follow the family occupation. As far as I could tell, Digger was like any other plumber—sort of grimy, with shaggy, light brown hair sticking out from under his baseball-style cap. He wasn't tall, but his arms bulged with muscles. At least he wore overalls, not droopy work pants that showed the proverbial "plumber's crack."

Digger's "way back sometime" question brought up a topic I didn't want to discuss. After all, Digger had lived in Warner Pier a lot longer than I had, and it was a town of only twenty-five hundred. He ought to know more about the Bailey house and the Bailey family than I did.

So I dodged the question.

"I don't know much about the house's history," I said. "And I didn't know the Baileys very well, but my aunt says they were wonderful neighbors. I'm afraid that since they'd both been ill during the past few years, they hadn't maintained the place too well. The two kids are selling it as is."

There. Maybe that would get Digger back on the topic. Which was the house's plumbing, not its history.

Instead, it led to a different nosy question. "I guess these houses along Lake Shore Drive are selling for a bunch of money. What are you planning to ask when you flip it?"

I gave a deep, annoyed sigh and hoped Digger heard it. "That depends on how much it costs for the renovations," I said. "Such as the plumbing. We're relying on you to tell us that."

Digger grunted as he bounced the beam of his flashlight around the concrete walls and floor of the unfinished basement.

The overhead light was on, but its bulb was dim, and the corners of the room were murky.

The house had been built in the mid-'50s, according to Joe and Hogan. Genuine "mid-century modern," they called it. It was one story, with an open floor plan. It had an attached carport on its north side, a wall of glass in the living room, and exposed rafters in the kitchen. Those rafters were ornamental, not utilitarian like the rafters Digger and I were looking at in the basement. All the house lacked was a flat roof; Joe said it might have had one originally, but the lake-effect snows of the Lake Michigan shore had apparently proved such a roof impractical, and at some point a slanted one had been installed.

"I'll do some figuring before I make an estimate," Digger said. "That is, if you want a firm price."

"Naturally," I said. Talk about stating the obvious. What else would we want? A shaky price?

I resisted the temptation to hit the guy. Or at least to snarl at him.

I was ready to hit anybody these days, and it wasn't Digger's fault. I wasn't really mad at him; I was mad at the two most important men in my life, Joe and Hogan.

I'm Lee Woodyard, a Texas gal who wound up living "up North," in a resort town on Lake Michigan. This happened because I became business manager for my aunt, an expert chocolatier who owned a shop specializing in luxury bonbons and truffles—the kind of chocolate that appeals to the rich folks who live in or who visit a resort like Warner Pier, Michigan.

Five years earlier I had moved to Warner Pier—my mother's hometown and the most picturesque resort on Lake Michigan. I had planned to stay only a couple of years, but to my surprise,

I had found myself putting down roots. I had even fallen in love with a great guy who was a native Michiganian. Joe Woodyard and I had been married three years and now lived in a hundred-year-old house built by my great-grandfather.

We got the family home when my aunt, Nettie TenHuis, remarried after several years of widowhood—linking up with another great guy named Hogan Jones. Hogan just happened to be chief of police for our town, and he and Joe were friends as well as in-laws. Hogan and Aunt Nettie moved into a house Hogan owned, and they passed Aunt Nettie's house on to us.

This was all fine until Joe and Hogan had the brilliant idea of flipping a house. Both had experience with building projects, and they thought they could have fun and make some money. When the house down the lane from Joe and me went on the market, they declared it the perfect opportunity and put in an offer. Aunt Nettie, an eternal optimist, thought it was a lovely plan. Everybody was happy but me. I hated the idea.

Joe and I had to mortgage a debt-free house to raise our share of the money. Everything in my soul, character, and personality yelled, "Wait a minute!"

I made it clear to Joe, Hogan, and Aunt Nettie that I hated the idea. They all claimed to understand why I felt that way. But they went ahead anyway, dragging me into the deal with them. And I hated the idea even more after another bidder appeared. Spud Dirk, a small-time developer in Warner Pier, said he was going to come up with a better bid for the property. Spud's idea was to build a complex of vacation apartments, a proposal that did not thrill Joe and me. We liked our neighborhood the way it was, a rural area abutting a neglected orchard that Spud already owned. I didn't see why Spud Dirk couldn't just sell his orchard, take the profit, and leave our neighborhood in its current state.

But the Bailey kids were holding to our handshake deal, telling Spud Dirk they'd already promised to sell to us. This thrilled Joe and Hogan, and even Aunt Nettie. It infuriated Spud, apparently, since he threatened to punch Joe out over it. When I heard about that, Joe said, "Spud talks a lot." The two of them never exchanged anything but words about the house.

So the four of us were in the process of buying the Bailey house, and the Bailey kids were allowing us to go into the house and get ready for the remodeling even before the papers were signed.

Everything was great, except that I hadn't slept for a week.

"Now, Lee," Joe had said, "I promise. Hogan and I will handle everything. You will simply keep on with your usual activities. You won't have to pound a nail or pick a paint color."

"I'm not afraid of the work," I said. "I'm afraid to borrow money."

"But the potential for making a big profit by flipping the Bailey house is just lying there. Between us, Hogan and I have enough experience—"

"No! I know y'all can remodel the house, Joe! You just can't do it without borrowing money. And our only collarbone—I mean, collateral! Our only collateral is our own home."

I'm one of those people who get their words mixed up— such as by swapping "collarbone" and "collateral." Luckily, people close to me, such as my husband, mostly ignore my twisted tongue.

I pushed right on with my argument. "And you know how I hate to borrow money."

Joe went right on, too. "Lee, you're an accountant and an excellent businesswoman. You're aware that sometimes you have to borrow money to make money."

"No," I said.

I was falling back on my favorite method of arguing. Just state your position. Don't bring up a lot of reasons. When your opponent can tear down arguments one at a time, you lose. If you simply stick to your decision, you can win. So I kept repeating, "No."

Joe was the one arguing. "If I could make a nice chunk of money," he said, "I could put it toward my debt."

That's where he had me. Mortgage and all.

Joe's first marriage—ending in a divorce and the subsequent death of his ex-wife—had left him deeply in debt. He now worked two jobs—one running a boat-restoration business and one as an attorney—to keep even. Yes, a large infusion of cash would be a major help to our personal finances.

I had finally agreed to go along with flipping the house. But I refused to be gracious about it.

And despite all Joe's promises that I wouldn't have to help with the project, there I was, showing the plumber the house so we could get an estimate on that part of the construction. And doing it at a time when I should be at work. My own work. Selling chocolate. I glanced at my watch. I had an appointment at four o'clock, this one to confer on a community project. Was I going to be late?

I had already been late meeting Digger, leaving him to twiddle his thumbs in the carport until I could get there. Or he should have been twiddling his thumbs.

Actually he could have gotten in on his own, or so he said.

He'd already told me that his brother knew the Baileys' son, Tad, and that all the "gang" of guys they ran around with in high school used this basement as a hangout.

"Mrs. Bailey left a key hidden by the outside door for them," Digger said. "She used to lock the door at the top of the stairs instead. Of course, I was a kid brother. I wasn't supposed to come in that way, but I knew about it."

Digger had assured me that everybody in rural Michigan hid a key near their cellar door. "I remembered where this one was because I knew the Baileys when I was a kid," he said. "Mr. Bailey kept a key on a rafter in the carport in those days, and I'll bet it's still there."

"That so?" I sighed. I didn't want to hear about the Baileys' basement door key.

The whole afternoon was leaving me a bit exasperated anyway. I told myself that as soon as I was at my desk, I was going to comfort myself with a caramel shark. Flavored, oddly enough, with sea salt.

Every year our little resort, Warner Pier, picks a theme for the summer's tourism projects and advertising. This year it had been "Lake Michigan—Fisherman's Paradise." Decorations and special events had all focused on native fish.

And, of course, the native fish of Lake Michigan do not include sharks. But the plan had worked. We had sold bunches—schools—of fishy chocolates, all flavored with hints of salt.

When Aunt Nettie suggested that we create and sell chocolate sharks in several flavors, all using a smidgeon of sea salt to bring out their sweetness, I thought she must have been having nightmares. But when she made some samples, I was won over from the first bite.

Our promotional material described my favorite flavor as having "a soft caramel center enrobed with milk chocolate, with bits of sea salt embellishing the top."

I tried to listen to Digger, but in my imagination I could taste that soft caramel. It tasted delicious without sticking to my teeth.

Digger was rattling on. "I kinda like these old basements," he said. "My grandmother's house had a cellar door like this one does. Does your house, over there across the road, have one?"

"No. We don't have an outside door into the basement. But we have a Michigan basement."

"Good old sand floors?"

"Right."

"Well, either kind of basement looks homier if it has a big bag of potatoes propped in the corner. Does the one over at your house have these thick walls?"

"Not as thick as these. About a foot."

"Not much good for storage, then. Not like this one."

The Bailey house had concrete walls about two feet thick. Since the rafters were open, there were lots of niches available for storing stuff. Old fruit jars, rarely used cleaning materials, and odd gadgets proliferated in these rooms, filling the space on the tops of the walls. Joe, Hogan, Aunt Nettie, and I had spent a lot of time clearing this one out.

At least Digger's questions had stopped for the moment. He was quiet as he picked up the ladder he had brought along and propped it against the wall, settling the legs firmly on the floor.

"These pipes are for the bathroom," he said. "I hope they haven't leaked over the years."

"That's why we called you in, Digger. You're supposed to tell us if they have to be replaced."

"When was this house built? In the 1950s?"

"That's right."

I deliberately kept my answer short. I didn't want to encourage Digger to come up with any more questions, time-consuming questions. I peeked at my watch. Three o'clock. *Darn! I ought to be at the office.*

Digger's voice brought me back to the current problem. "I guess the Baileys left this stuff here."

"Stuff? What stuff? We thought we cleared everything out."

Digger used his flashlight to point at some rags tucked away on the niche that topped the concrete wall.

"You shouldn't leave this here," he said. "It's bound to attract mice."

"Gross! Pull it out, Digger. Let's get that out of here. There are some trash sacks in the kitchen." I headed for the wooden steps that led upstairs.

"There's something wrapped up in them," Digger said.

"What is it?" I turned around, stopping halfway up the stairs to look at him. As I watched, he juggled the rags around, grabbing at the bundle. He made a final snatch, but missed, and the wad of rags landed at the foot of his ladder.

I hadn't expected it to make such a loud noise when it hit.

And I hadn't expected to feel the wind as a bullet flew past me and buried itself in the concrete wall.

Chapter 2

The noise was stunning. It reverberated off the concrete walls and shook the wooden rafters. I'm sure the whole house vibrated from the sound, that the walls and the ceilings lost some nails, and that the roof must have dropped shingles in all directions.

It sure shook Digger and me. He slipped off his ladder, landing on his knees, and the ladder fell backward, ending up on top of him. I sat down hard, coming close to smashing my tailbone as my fanny plunked onto a wooden step.

But we reacted fast. Digger threw the ladder aside and scrambled to his feet. His lips were moving, though I couldn't hear a thing he said. I stood up, then covered my ears with my hands and wagged my head from side to side. There was no use talking until the sound stopped bouncing around inside my head. I think I mouthed the words, "I'm okay," but a loud ringing noise kept me from hearing anything. The smell of gunpowder seeped into my nose.

Digger looked terrified. His mouth kept moving, and after what seemed like ten minutes but was probably only two, I began to understand what he was saying. It was, "You're bleeding!"

I checked then and realized that my arm had been scratched, but the wound didn't amount to much. I was sure it had come from a flying concrete chip.

"I'm okay," I said again. "Just a scratch." By then my voice sounded as if I were in an echo chamber.

I found a Kleenex in my pocket and dabbed at the spot on my arm. That's when I began to shake. I guess that was the moment I realized that either Digger or I could have been seriously hurt. Like killed.

Anyway, Digger was abjectly apologizing for dropping a gun, and I was feeling luckier and luckier because the bullet whizzed by both of us without hitting anything but a concrete wall. He swore he wasn't hurt by his fall off his ladder.

In a few minutes we got ourselves together. I was still shaky, but I joined Digger to look at the pistol. It had landed at the foot of his ladder, and the gun was now lying there looking innocent. Both of us leaned over it, putting our heads together and peering closely. Neither of us made a move toward touching it; I think we felt as if it might go off again, and that we'd better be ready to take cover.

Digger picked up his flashlight from the floor and spotlighted the pistol. My first impression was that some outlaw from the Old West must have abandoned the weapon in the Baileys' basement. It was a long-barreled pistol with a metal handle. An old-fashioned six-shooter.

I can't really describe it much better. Some people think a woman from Texas ought to know all about guns, but the only firearms I've ever been around were my dad's deer rifles. Pistols are a complete mystery to me. I've never even fired one.

"Well," I said, "I guess the Baileys forgot their gun."

"I guess so," Digger said. "But what was it doing in the rafters of the basement?"

And that, of course, was the first mystery. But it seemed easily solved. I told Digger either Joe or I would call the Baileys' daughter—the person who was handling the details of the sale of the house for the family—and tell her we found a pistol. She could probably explain how it came to be there and tell us what to do with it.

Digger looked at me sideways. "Are you going to tell Hogan Jones about this?"

"I'll probably mention it. After all, we've had an abduction. I mean, an adventure!"

My wrong word seemed to fly right over Digger's head. "I'm still scared to death when I think how close that bullet came to you," he said.

"The whole thing was a pure accident, Digger." I laughed. "I promise not to file charges."

"If I'd realized it was a gun before I picked it up—well, I sure would have handled it different. But all I saw was a wad of rags."

"I expected you to pull out a dead mouse. That might have been more gruesome. I doubt we'll forget this, but let's move on."

Digger picked up the pistol, handling it gingerly and pointing it away from both of us. I found a plastic trash sack up in the kitchen, and he put the pistol in it, along with the rags it had been wrapped in.

After he finished his survey of the plumbing, he carried the pistol over to my house, I cleared a place to put it in the broom closet, and I locked the kitchen door as we left. I guess we both still felt as if the pistol might go off again, even without any encouragement. Such as dropping it onto its hammer. That's what Digger seemed to think had caused the bang.

Digger left, still apologizing. But to my relief he didn't say anything more about the Bailey house being connected to a long-ago crime.

Sometime in there I found a moment to call my assistant, Bunny Birdsong, to tell her I was going to be late for my appointment. It was almost four o'clock when I finally got to my office. Maggie McNutt, one of my best friends, was waiting.

"Sorry I'm late," I said. "Did Bunny give you a shark?"

"She gave me two, and I already ate one." Maggie held up a Dark and Stormy truffle. "According to your list of flavors, it's 'a dark chocolate center flavored with sea salt, then enrobed with dark chocolate and embellished with chopped pecans.'"

"Good choice," I said. "I'll have a Caramel Shark with sea salt. I've been craving one all afternoon."

I reached for the stash I kept in my drawer, and we both bit into yummy chocolate and made happy noises.

Maggie already knew why TenHuis Chocolade had decided to make truffles in the shape of sharks. Lake Michigan doesn't have any native sharks. Probably because the Great Lakes contain only freshwater. But the whole world, not only Lake Michigan tourism, was crazy for sharks that summer. It started, as so many parts of popular culture do, with a television show, in which gorgeous guys and girls—who in actuality must have spent half their lives in the gym—interacted with sharks. Don't ask what the two species did; it was both scary and titillating, and it quickly became a top-rated show.

One of Michigan's slogans is "Lake Michigan—Unsalted and Shark Free." But that summer TenHuis had sharks, chocolate ones with salt on top. All the locals thought it was a great joke.

As I ate my shark-shaped truffle-bodied shark, I looked around my new office with satisfaction. Aunt Nettie and I had expanded the TenHuis Chocolade shop the previous winter, doubling its size by buying the building next door. Then we went through a remodeling project, which like all such projects took twice as long and was twice as expensive as expected.

Now it made me feel good to look around at the finished product, admiring the new black-and-white floor, the comfy chairs for waiting customers, the nonslip workroom floor, and the sophisticated decor in the shop.

Then I turned to Maggie. "Okay. What are you up to this time?" Maggie is the drama teacher at the local high school, and she's always full of ideas to help her students learn and to win praise and prizes for them. And she expects her friends to help her accomplish this.

Maggie smiled winningly. "I've got an idea for the Warner Pier Summer Showboat."

"Oh? But the Showboat folded—what? Four years ago?"

"Yep. I think it's about time to revive it. It would be the perfect site for a drama camp for high schoolers and college students."

"I wish you luck," I said. "But what do you want me to do about it?"

"The first thing I need is some money."

"Can't help you there, gal. Joe's tied all ours up."

"No! No! I don't want *your* money. I want a grant. Maybe from the VHD Foundation. If I can put you on the advisory committee, and you can help me with the application, it would really make a difference."

I made a noncommittal noise, and Maggie kept talking.

"I know it will be a big job," she said. "I don't see any alternative to leasing the building. And I can't do that without financial support. And having an organization with an advisory committee at my back would make me look a lot more respectable."

The Warner Pier Summer Showboat wasn't really a boat; it was a theater that sat beside the river in an abandoned warehouse on the edge of Warner Pier's downtown. The seats, the curtains, and some of the lighting and sound equipment were still there, Maggie reported. She said a builder had checked it out. The estimate for refurbishing and partially reequipping the theater made me feel only slightly sick to my stomach.

"Oh, Maggie!" I said. "Wouldn't you be just as happy financing a moon launch? It would cost about the same amount."

Maggie looked disappointed, so I quickly reassured her. "Of course, I'll help you any way I can. What's the first step?"

"I thought it would be writing a proposal for the VHD Foundation."

I had to agree. It's hard to get anything done in Warner Pier without the VanHorn-Davis Foundation. A family foundation, the VHD is well over seventy-five years old and is definitely the most influential such agency in our part of Michigan. And probably the richest, too.

I agreed to help Maggie with the grant application, and she handed over a sheaf of background material. And after one more truffle each, our meeting ended. Maggie's optimism was infecting me. I felt quite enthusiastic as she shut the door behind herself.

At least that episode had made me think about something besides a pistol going off in a basement.

I checked in with Aunt Nettie, the boss of TenHuis Chocolade, but I resisted the temptation to tell her all about the accident at the Bailey house. I decided to tell Joe first. For one thing, Joe had the phone number of the Baileys' daughter, and I thought she was the person we needed to call about the gun.

Joe is definitely one of the top three best-looking guys in west Michigan, with shoulders that are first on the list. At six-one, he's a shade taller than I am, and he mixes black hair and bright blue eyes into a sexy combination. By the time Joe came home that evening, I had created a dramatic story about the gun in the basement. It featured me as a brave woman who handled the whole event with calmness and authority, but I added a few laugh lines.

I was a tiny bit disappointed when Joe didn't enjoy the tale. In fact, he got rather upset. He demanded to see my arm. He threatened to punch Digger out. He walked back and forth and raised his voice. It took quite a while to calm him down. Then we walked over to the Bailey house so Joe could see the scene.

At least it was a pleasant fall evening, just right for a short walk.

In a way Warner Pier wraps up Michigan's history. It was founded before the Civil War, when Michigan was producing lots and lots of lumber. Chicago couldn't have been built without lumber from west Michigan, or so we tell everyone. Eventually the whole state of Michigan became almost bare of trees as early settlers felled forests, then shipped the wood across the Great Lakes for building supplies.

Then Michiganians—or Michiganders if you prefer—began

to replant trees again. But this time Michigan turned to fruit trees. Our part of the state became a major fruit-producing area. Cherries, peaches, apples—plus blueberries, which grow on bushes, not trees, but which sure add to the yum factor. Michigan may be known for producing cars and trucks and have plenty of light and heavy industry, but farming isn't a minor part of the economy.

Neither is tourism, and that's where our particular town excels. More than a hundred years ago people in Chicago and other cities of the Upper Midwest discovered the beaches of Lake Michigan, and Warner Pier became a resort.

Even today our town is divided into three kinds of people: locals, tourists, and summer people. Locals, such as Joe and me, live there year-round. Tourists come for a few days or a couple of weeks. Summer people own or lease property and make extended stays. The three classes mix and mingle, come and go.

We locals love the tourists and summer people because they bring money and leave it behind in our businesses. And they pay taxes. Every day we should say prayers of thanks for the tourists and summer people.

Warner Pier has also become an art colony, with galleries, a small theater (in addition to the Showboat that Maggie was thinking of reopening), recitals, and other displays of cultural interest. Add in the beautiful beaches, the lush forests—native trees are back, as well as the orchards—the pleasant summer weather, and the interesting old houses, and it adds up to an idyllic summer resort.

Joe and I love it. Our farmhouse-style house is just a quarter of a mile from the lake. Yes, it gets a bit cold here in the wintertime, but we can stand that.

Those beautiful woods and waters are probably the factors that led Joe and Hogan to decide to flip a house. Property values are high in our neighborhood. And since our neighborhood is semirural, the lots are at least a couple of acres in size, though some small-housing additions are being developed.

I could see the shabby condition of the Bailey house as we reached the carport. The main value of the property was in the land. Anything with an address on Lake Shore Drive is high-dollar in our area.

I would agree that flipping this particular house was a good idea if it hadn't been for the mortgage on our house that went along with the deal.

My thoughts made me sigh deeply. Joe sighed, too, then put his arm around my shoulders. I sighed again. I saw the signs of another pep talk on its way, and I didn't want to hear it.

"Lee," Joe said, "I'm really convinced—"

I interrupted him. "We've chewed that topic to a rag. I've got a different subject to discuss."

"Go on."

"Digger asked me a question I couldn't answer, but one I've heard hints about from other people."

"What was that?"

"He asked if the Bailey house hadn't been connected with a crime."

Joe didn't reply, unless you count taking his arm from around my shoulders a reply.

Then he laughed.

I stopped walking and turned to look at him. "Joe! Was there a murder or something here?"

"No! No!"

"Whew! You scared me. If I find out we've bought a house that's known around town as the Abode of the Damned, I'm going to be mad."

Joe laughed. "No, it's nothing like that. It was some boys in the neighborhood. They pulled a dumb stunt. One of them was the Baileys' son. But it got more laughs than notoriety. And it did not happen at this location."

Youthful problems. I could deal with that. I gave another sigh, this one of relief. "Okay, Joe. What did the neighborhood boys do?"

Joe looked down, kicked a rock, and cleared his throat again. "It was a sort of a mix-up. Just a prank."

"Joe! You are dodging the question, and it's making me nervous. Just tell me what happened."

"They were suspected of robbing a convenience store."

Chapter 3

I stared at Joe. "Robbing a convenience store?"

He didn't look at me.

"Joe! That's a serious crime."

Joe nodded.

"Joe . . ."

"Listen," he said. "Let's look at the basement. Then I'll tell you the whole story. At least as much as I know. It was just a kids' stunt."

He took a step toward the basement door, but I grabbed his arm. "Joe! When did this happen?"

"When I was a junior in high school."

Dread filled me. "Joe, you weren't involved, were you?"

He laughed. "Nope. I've even got an alibi. I was at a wrestling camp in Kalamazoo. Of course, I knew all the guys involved."

"Knew them well?"

"Lee! This happened in Warner Pier. Population two thousand five hundred. I assure you I knew everybody in the whole high school well. I'll tell you about it after we look at the basement."

I considered pitching a fit and refusing to go into the basement until he told me what had happened. But I wanted the whole story, not an abbreviated version.

"Okay," I said. "But you're not getting out of it. I want to know."

"I promise. I'll tell all. Or all I know."

When we went into the Bailey house, Joe asked for a detailed explanation of how the pistol came to be fired. Where was I standing? Where was Digger's ladder? He carefully examined the spot where the bullet hit the cement wall.

I finally balked. "Joe, I'm hungry. Let's go home before the meat loaf is baked as dry as a bone."

"I just wanted to understand exactly what happened," he said.

"Come home," I said. "I'm beginning to think you don't want to talk about the whole thing."

When we got to the dinner table, he became quiet, staring silently at his plate of meat loaf.

"Who?" I asked.

"Who what?"

"Who was involved in the convenience store robbery that wasn't really a crime? And didn't really happen at the Bailey house?"

Joe gave a deep sigh and picked up his fork. "Well, Digger's brother was, for one."

"What? If Digger's brother was involved, why was Digger asking me? He should just ask Chip."

"Digger was probably trying to figure out how much you know. Digger was a bratty younger brother at that time. Chip probably didn't tell him anything. Actually all the Sharks have been fairly closemouthed about exactly what happened."

"The Sharks?"

"Yep. That's what the guys called themselves."

"That's a coincidence!" I said, thinking of our adorable chocolate sharks. "Were the Sharks cute guys? Because our cute little chocolate sharks are a huge hit."

"How the heck would I know who was a cute guy?"

"Never mind. Who was in this gang?"

"Chip Brown. Plus Sharpy Brock. Tad Bailey. Spud Dirk—"

"Spud? The guy who's trying to buy the Bailey house?"

"Right."

"Chip, Sharpy, Tad, and Spud? Were the members required to have silly names? And why did they call themselves sharks, anyway?"

"I don't know. I think they copied the name from *West Side Story*."

"I've never met any of them. Except Digger."

"Digger was too young to be part of the gang. It was his brother Chip, plus Sharpy, Spud, and Tad. The five Sharks."

"Even though there were only four of them?"

"Oh, I guess I left one out. Did I mention Buzz? Brad Davis?"

"Brad Davis? As in the ramrod of the VanHorn-Davis Foundation?"

"Yep. That very person."

I stared in disbelief. "You've got to be kidding."

"Why should I be? In those days Brad Davis was a regular human being. His father hadn't yet bought him a halo."

"Maggie and I were talking about the VanHorn-Davis Foundation this afternoon."

Joe looked incredulous. "What on earth for?"

I briefly sketched Maggie's plan to form an organization and lease the old Showboat Theater for a drama camp.

Joe nodded. "That sounds like a VHD kind of project, turning it into a camp for high schoolers. It will have to sound virtuous, though, not like a summer job for Maggie."

"Oh, I realize that. The *V* in the foundation's name doesn't really stand for 'Van.' It means 'Virtue.' That's why it's quite surprising to hear that one of the clan would be a robber. Even a fake one."

"Actually Brad wasn't a rob-ber. He was a rob-bee."

I gave a deep sigh. "Okay, Joe. Cough it up. I have to know the whole story. And what did it have to do with the Bailey house?"

"It had nothing to do with the Bailey house directly. The Baileys were just being nice to their son's friends. They let the boys use part of the basement as a clubhouse.

"I was there once or twice. They had an old refrigerator, an older TV set, and a junky couch. Honestly, Lee, these were perfectly nice guys, or the Baileys wouldn't have let them hang around."

"Then what's the story on the holdup?"

"The story is simply a high school prank gone wrong."

And as Joe told it, that was all it was. But it doesn't make sense without an understanding of the VHD Foundation. And that history starts 175 years ago.

That's when a New England missionary named Cyrus Davis was sent to west Michigan to minister to the settlers and to proselytize among the Indians. Cyrus's efforts were quite successful; he founded a half-dozen churches and a college before he died in the early 1900s. His son married a VanHorn girl, a member of a Dutch immigrant family who had become wealthy merchants in the area.

It seemed that everyone in both families prospered. Orchards, industry, tourism—they were involved in everything that makes a business successful in our area. If the Davises didn't have a finger in the pie, then the VanHorns did. They also excelled at the more prosperous professions—law, medicine, architecture. Even our county's most successful funeral home is VanHorn Family Funeral Services.

In fact, when Joe joked about Brad Davis and his halo, he was talking about all the VanHorn-Davis family members. They were regarded as the patron saints of the region. Oh, I suppose that some Davis or some VanHorn had once done something naughty. But the word didn't get around.

Envy and other human flaws often make members of prominent families targets of gossip and suspicion, but the Davises and the VanHorns had remained largely above such feelings. I'd always believed it was because of the VHD Foundation.

The foundation was established just after World War II, and its purpose was to coordinate the charitable activities of the merged family. "Making Giving Effective," its motto read.

That was certainly a goal a business manager like me could understand. And the VHD Foundation had succeeded almost too well. Sometimes I felt the organization was turning into a community dictator. If VHD wanted a project, it went over. If they didn't want it, it went down.

The organization's top priority was culture. Then came education, economic growth, and charity.

I had to admit a lot of our area's success is because of the VHD. They built the theaters and auditoriums, endowed university chairs, paid summer interns, supported NPR stations, financed school facilities, funded food banks, and handed out college scholarships.

All these are good things for a community. And as long as the community goals matched the ideas of the current board of the VHD Foundation, all went well.

But the Texan in me had always been a bit suspicious of unmitigated virtue.

Bradley "Buzz" Davis certainly seemed to be an exemplar of the family traits. Joe and I knew him and his wife, Felicia, fairly well. Brad had graduated from Warner Pier High School—the Davises and VanHorns were egalitarian in education, so they made sure the local schools met high scholastic standards—and went on to Yale, then got an MBA from Harvard. He now managed many of the family's business interests.

And he was president of the VHD Foundation. That job made him one of the most important men in west Michigan.

The high school armed robbery that got the Sharks into trouble started with Brad, Joe said.

"Brad's dad was determined that his son wasn't going to be one of those snobby rich kids," Joe said. "So he made Brad get a summer job."

The job was clerking in a convenience store. After Joe revealed that to me, he stopped talking and again stared at his meat loaf, apparently not wanting to go on.

"And?" I said. "What happened?"

"In a way Brad brought the whole thing on himself."

"The whole thing? What whole thing?"

"It's really silly, Lee."

"I don't care! Tell me."

Joe gave a deep sigh. "Brad got assigned to work the night shift."

"So?"

"So, one of the other Sharks referred to the convenience store as a 'stop-n-rob.'"

"I've heard them called that."

"We all have. But the term made Brad think about the possibility of being held up. He began to obsess about it."

"It's certainly something to be cautious about, in that sort of store. I mean, they're open late and are often in lonely neighborhoods."

"True. But Brad showed his fears a little too plainly. His buddies caught on."

"And they let him have it?"

"Right. Brad began to be the butt of jokes. All about holding up the store."

"Poor guy! And there wasn't much he could do about it."

"Actually he did take action. Brad dug a pistol out of the family attic or something."

"He didn't!"

"He did. He took it to work with him and hid it under the counter. I guess it made him feel secure. Or it did until the night that the guys showed up."

"The robbers?"

"Nope. Not real robbers. It was Sharpy, Spud, Tad, and Chip—all rigged out in hoodies, with bandannas covering their faces. They waited until the store was empty of customers, then burst in the door, yelling and brandishing weapons."

"Real weapons?"

"Actually I think that between them they had two BB pistols and a couple of toy guns. But the weapons looked real."

"Oh my gosh! When they came in Brad must have fainted dead away."

"Not at all. He simply reached under the counter, pulled out the pistol he'd hidden there, and brandished it back. Bullets—and BBs—began to fly."

"Wow! Was anybody hurt?"

Joe chuckled. "Nope. But the Frozen Rainbow machine took a direct hit."

Chapter 4

I began to laugh, of course.

The thought of gallons of sticky, icy liquid covering the floor of a convenience store, of Sharks flying into the air and landing flat on their fannies, of everything colored bright red, blue, and yellow—it was simply hilarious.

At least it was funny to someone who didn't have to clean it up. It wasn't so funny to think of how sticky the mess would have been and of finding yellow or red goo under the counters months later or of people getting hurt when they fell.

I knew how maddening it was to clean up chocolate, and sticky, icky Frozen Rainbow gunk might have been a worse job.

But I didn't have to do the scrubbing and mopping or witness the falls, so I laughed, and Joe joined in. We finished our dinner with laughter bubbling through the dining room.

Then the phone rang. I answered, and I wasn't surprised to hear Hogan's voice. I *was* surprised to hear what he had to say.

"Lee!" He sounded gruff, which was unusual. "What's this about a shooting out there?"

I took a couple of breaths before I answered. I hadn't told

Aunt Nettie about finding the pistol, so how had Hogan found out?

"Well," I said. "Nobody was hurt."

"Why didn't you tell me about it?"

"Since it was only an acrobat—I mean an accident! It was only an accident, and nobody was hurt, so I didn't think we had to report it to the police. I just got around to telling Joe about it a little while ago."

"I'm more concerned that you found a stray gun."

"I was going to ask Joe for the number of the Bailey girl—the one who is handling the sale of her parents' house. She ought to know something about the gun. If she doesn't, then we should turn it in to law enforcement, I guess. Joe will know what the law is. Can't you ask the feds if there's a connection between a certain weapon and a crime?"

"Only with a specific crime. Not to a general listing of crimes. Hey, is Joe there?"

"Sure." I handed Joe the phone, and he punched the speaker button. "Yah?"

"Joe, I've got a question about something from Warner Pier's history. Do you remember the date when that crazy holdup that wasn't a holdup happened at the Country Convenience Store?"

"Not off the top of my head! Just that it was the July before I was a junior in high school," Joe said. "And why on earth would anyone need to know that at this late date?"

"Digger's been talking about the gun around town," Hogan said. "One of the old-timers remembered something odd about it."

"I could figure it out by looking at the *Gazette*."

"Oh, wow," I said. "It made the newspaper?"

Joe shook his head. "No, Lee. I'm sure the Davis family was able to keep it out of print. But something much more noteworthy happened that night that did hit the news. Meyer 'Curley' McWhirley died."

Hogan replied with a "Hmmm," but I snorted with laughter.

"You're kidding," I said. "No real person could be named Curley McWhirley."

"Oh, he was a real person," Joe said. "One of the town nuts. I thought you'd remember him, Hogan."

"Nope. I didn't move to Warner Pier until a few years after you graduated from high school. So? Was this Curley guy important?"

"Not to this story. But he regularly raised a ruckus in Warner Pier."

"How? Was he an unpopular mayor?"

Joe chuckled. "He wasn't a mayor at all. M-e-y-e-r was his first name. Pronounced like the title of a city official. 'Mayor.' Anyway, he lived not far from the Country Convenience Store, maybe a mile farther south on Lake Shore Drive. He had curly hair, and he didn't like to be teased about it, so he shaved his head. He was one of those people who get up at every meeting and start out, 'I object.' No matter what other people wanted to do, he objected."

"So people noticed when he died? Was it natural causes?"

"Oh yes. He'd had heart surgery, and the cardiologist told him he had to walk every day, or else. So, every night after dinner ol' Curley collected his flashlight and took a walk." Joe shook his head. "The joke was that everybody except his wife and his doctor knew that he was walking to the convenience store to get a large-sized Hershey bar."

Hogan gave a deep sigh. "One of those, huh?"

"Right. So his death wasn't unexpected. But even though the death was perfectly natural, it got a lot more attention than some teenage prank. If you want to know the exact date, it should be easy to find in the *Gazette* files."

"I'll check the records," Hogan said. "I don't like it when stray pistols turn up in my bailiwick."

Joe chuckled. "Wherever the gun in the Bailey house came from, it had nothing to do with Curley. He had a heart attack. I suppose the gun might link to the prank holdup in some way. But it seems more likely to me that it was a pistol the Baileys had and for some reason they forgot it when they moved out."

"When were you going to call the Bailey girl about the gun?"

"I didn't know I was until I just heard Lee mention it. But Twyla McDonald—that's her married name—she lives on the West Coast now. I can call her as soon as I find her number. It's still early out there."

"Let me know what she says, please. And, Lee?"

"I'm here."

"I'm going to run out to the Bailey house tomorrow morning. I might ask you to show me where you found the gun."

"Fine. I'm off until noon. I'll be around."

We both hung up then, but Hogan's questions had given me something to think about. "Joe, what happened to all the Sharks?"

"Oh, they went their separate ways. I'm not sure I know where all of them are now. I think Chip Brown became an electrician. He may be in the Detroit area."

"And Digger wasn't a member of the gang?"

"No. Digger was five years younger. The Sharks would have thought he was just a kid."

"How about Tad Bailey? He's in the army, right?"

"He went in as soon as he was out of high school. Twyla said he's in for the long haul. He lives in Oklahoma. And we already talked about Brad Davis. He's become a big dog."

"Who were the other two? I've already forgotten their names."

"Sharpy Brock. He went to Michigan State. Got a couple of graduate degrees. I think he teaches in a college someplace."

"And the other one must have been Spud. Right?"

"Right. The one who threatened to punch me out over buying the Bailey house. But we're getting the house with no blows exchanged." Joe frowned. "Now I have a question for you. Why?"

"Why what?"

"Why do you want to know?"

I thought about the question before I tried to answer.

"I don't have the slightest idea why I wanted to know," I said. "Maybe I just wondered if I knew any of the guys. Or maybe it's just my curiosity bump bothering me, as usual. And now, how about some ice cream?"

Joe did call Twyla McDonald (née Bailey) as soon as we'd finished dessert, but she didn't answer. And she didn't return his call that evening. We went to bed still not knowing anything more about how a pistol that Wyatt Earp might have carried managed to appear in the basement of a mid-century modern house in Michigan. In fact, the last words Joe said before he fell asleep were, "I was really sure we got all the junk out of that basement."

When Hogan showed up the next morning, about an hour after Joe had left for his law office in Holland, I invited him in for a cup of coffee partly so I could ask that question.

"How did an Old West six-shooter wind up in the Baileys' basement?"

Hogan laughed before he answered. "May I see the pistol?"

I handed him the plastic sack we had stored it in. "It's just that it looks so historic," I said. "As if it's so old it should be in a museum."

Still chuckling, Hogan took the pistol out of the sack and unwound the towels that covered it. "Yuk!" he said. "The thing's dirty enough to be a hundred years old."

Then he examined it. "It's a Colt Single Action Army pistol," he said. "People may call it the Peacemaker. They were manufactured beginning in 1873. But it's not really old."

"Well, 1873 sounds pretty old to me."

"This model was so popular that Colt manufactured thousands and thousands of them. They're still making them today. They've always been popular. Even after they weren't in general use by law enforcement, lots of people wanted one—reenactors, hobbyists, just people who thought it was fun to have a 'western' gun. This one has a serial number, which shows that it's more modern. Not an antique."

"Oh." I felt quite let down.

"I'll ask the National Crime Information Center if they know anything about this particular gun. If it's been reported stolen, they'll have a record of that. But there may not be anything in their records."

"It gave Digger and me quite a start."

"I'll bet it did. This model is notorious for going off unexpectedly. The old-time lawmen kept an empty chamber under the hammer for that very reason."

Hogan tucked the pistol back into its plastic sack. "Whenever you're ready I'll get you to show me where you were when the thing went off."

We walked over to the Bailey house, chatting idly about the problems of flipping it. We unlocked the front door and went through the house and down the basement stairs. Nothing had been moved or changed since Joe and I had been there the evening before.

I showed Hogan where Digger's ladder had been and where I'd been standing when the bullet whizzed past. He carefully examined the chip in the basement wall, but he didn't seem too impressed. No pictures were taken, no comments were made about calling the crime lab.

In fact, after we'd hashed and rehashed the episode thoroughly, Hogan seemed ready to go back to his office. But he headed for the house's kitchen door, not the front door we had entered.

"I'm going to take a minute to check out that carport," he said.

"I know you and Joe want to tear those cupboards out."

"Has Joe said how hard that would be?"

"Not to me."

"As long as we're here, I'll take a look at them."

I followed Hogan out the kitchen door, which opened into the carport. And I was hit by an odor, a smell that was powerful and unmistakable.

"Oh, ye gods! There's something dead out here." I cupped my hand over my nose and mouth. "Yuk!"

"I'll check it out," Hogan said. "I see the flies—whatever it is, it's in that back cupboard. You stay here."

I wasn't even tempted to follow him as he crossed the

carport. Now I remembered being aware of a slight but un-pleasant aroma as we approached the front door of the house. But this was impossible to ignore.

Hogan opened the door of the cupboard and turned on the light inside. He stood silently for a long moment before he spoke. "Lee, why don't you just go back to your house?"

"Why?"

"Because there's a body in here, and I don't think you need to look at it."

Chapter 5

I didn't argue.

If there's anything I don't care about seeing, it's a dead body a couple of days old. I won't go into exactly why I felt sure the body had been there a couple of days, but I was positive it had been.

I simply turned around and went to my own house. After I thought for a few moments, I went back outside, and I moved my van into the driveway of a neighbor who was out of town; I knew things were going to get crowded around the Bailey house and that our driveway would probably be blocked. I might not be able to get out, once all the law enforcement arrived.

I called Joe, who didn't answer, and I left a message on his cell phone. I called Aunt Nettie to warn her that I might not make it to the shop that afternoon. Actually I flat out told her I wouldn't make it to the shop. She promised to tell Bunny to fill in. She made sympathetic noises. Somehow I wasn't in the mood for sympathetic noises, and I hung up as quickly as I could.

By then the crowd was beginning to gather. I watched them from our living room windows.

At first the crowd was composed almost entirely of law

enforcement. The Warner Pier PD came first—all three of the officers in all three of the patrol cars. Then the Warner County sheriff and a couple of his prowl cars showed up. Next there was a contingent from the Michigan State Police. The state police don't just patrol the highways in Michigan. They also help small municipalities investigate serious crimes. A couple of their cars arrived, accompanied by the van that holds their portable lab.

The gang was all there. This wasn't the first time I'd seen a whole bunch of law enforcement officers respond to a serious crime. I've sometimes wondered, in my idle moments, if they all really need to be there or if they are simply curious. But trees blocked my view of the Bailey house. I couldn't tell what was going on over there. Maybe every single cop had an important job.

About an hour after I had started making calls, a lone figure came walking up the driveway. Joe had driven down from his Holland law office. Like me, he had parked in the neighbor's drive.

I was really glad to see Joe. I needed someone to put his arms around me for a while. And I needed to put my arms around someone. Namely Joe.

We took care of that matter quickly. With my head against his shoulder, I spoke in a muffled voice. "Joe, Hogan found a body in the cupboard of the Bailey house's carport."

"I know. He called to tell me. It was Spud Dirk."

"What!"

That was something of a shocker. Spud, of course, was the developer who had tried to buy the Bailey house, and when the Baileys stuck by our agreement to sell it to us, he'd made some ugly remarks to Joe about the whole situation. Publicly.

Joe spoke again. "Yah. The guy who cornered me at the post

office and reamed me out for wanting to buy the Bailey house."
He hugged me tighter.

"Who would want to kill him?"

"I have no idea.

"I can see him being mad because he didn't get the house,
but I don't see any connection between his disappointment and
somebody killing him." Joe took a couple of deep breaths, then
spoke again. "Hogan said he didn't think it was suicide."

"I didn't look at the body, but Hogan's reaction sure wasn't
like it was suicide. And every cop in west Michigan is here."

"Yah."

"You're sounding like a Dutchman."

Joe chuckled and held me tighter. "Can't help it, Texas gal.
I was born and bred in the Dutch patch."

West Michigan's original Dutch settlers have always had a
traditional way of pronouncing "yeah." They say "yah," like
the Dutch or German word for "yes." Joe's family came to this
area around 1890, so he isn't a descendant of the original Dutch
settlers, but nearly every native of west Michigan—no matter
what his background—says "yah."

Actually I'm the one who's a Dutch descendant—around
half-Dutch. But my mom ran off to Texas before I was born and
my dad was as Texan as a bluebonnet. I'd never heard a west
Michigan accent—except my mom's—until I was in my mid-
teens. So I pronounce "yeah" the way a Texan does. I say "yow."
Sometimes even "Shur-nuf."

I thought about that while Joe held me. It was a much more
pleasant subject than dead bodies in the carport cupboard.

Of course, after I had considered the proper pronunciation
of "yah" and "yow," and Joe and I had held each other for a

while, we both got curious. We went out onto the front porch and sat in lawn chairs. Even though our view was limited, we could tell there was a lot going on next door.

For the moment, none of it looked exciting. Occasionally a cop we knew drove or walked by and waved at us. But by mid-afternoon I was beginning to feel a bit slighted. After all, Joe and I were buying the property where the crime occurred. Or at least where the body had been dumped. Maybe we weren't owners of the crime scene yet, but it seemed as if we should merit some attention.

Then an ambulance came by, and the action seemed to pick up. A few cars left, and in about twenty minutes the ambulance went back out. We couldn't see into it, naturally. And about twenty minutes after that, Hogan and Sergeant Hal Haywood, one of the detectives of the Michigan State Police, walked up to our house.

We invited them in, and all of us went into the living room. Hal carefully laid a plastic zipper bag on the coffee table, and the men chatted while I made iced tea and handed it out. I put some truffles—three chocolate chip with sea salt and three French vanilla with sea salt—on a plate and put it on the coffee table. Then I sat on the couch and tried to look receptive to questions.

Hogan cleared his throat. "Well, I guess you two know enough to understand that the investigation has been handed over to Sergeant Haywood."

Joe nodded. "Sure," he said. "Since you are one of the potential owners of the house where the body was found, and you found the body, you're a little too closely connected with the whole thing to investigate it."

"Well, Joe, there's even more to it than that." Hogan

frowned. "One of my best friends, plus a relative—well, they're going to have to answer some questions."

"Huh?" Joe and I howled in unison.

"What's going on?" I asked.

"Who's involved?" Joe asked.

Hogan scrunched up his face, and Hal remained perfectly deadpan. But Hal was the one who spoke, and he spoke to Joe.

"Didn't you have an argument with Richard Dirk? An argument over buying the Bailey house?"

"Sure. Everybody in Warner Pier knows that. The traditional place to bump heads around here is the post office, and the two of us went at it in front of the boxes."

"Was there any more to it than that one run-in?"

"No, and I'd hardly call it a 'run-in.' We made a few sarcastic comments, then called it quits. I'm not going to punch a guy out unless he punches me first, or tries to. And Spud wasn't the kind of guy to throw a punch at all."

"Did you write him a threatening note?"

"You gotta be kidding! I'm a lawyer! We know better than to put threats in writing."

Hal frowned, but he didn't reply.

Joe leaned forward. "What's going on, Hal?"

Hal held up his plastic bag, pressing it flat so that the paper inside could be read. It wasn't large, just a scrap of lined paper, the sort a fourth grader might use. The top edge had been torn off.

Something had been printed on the paper. I leaned onto Joe's shoulder and together we read the words.

Get real. We're not giving up this idea. We have the

money, and we're buying the Bailey house. Get used to it. OR ELSE.

The note was signed in capital letters. "TATER."

Joe and I both stared at the note. Finally I spoke. "I'm all confused. Who the heck is Tater?"

"I haven't the slightest idea," Joe said. He tossed the plastic envelope back onto the table.

Haywood frowned. "I thought all of you had one of those nicknames. From your high school days."

"Dirk did," Joe said. "But it wasn't Tater. It was Spud. Everybody at Warner Pier High called him that. The Sharks' nicknames were not secret. Spud, Tad, Chip, Sharpy, and Buzz. Buzz—Brad Davis—has dropped his nickname, as far as I know. I don't know about the other guys."

Both Tater and Spud were slang terms for "potato." Weird coincidence.

"But I wasn't a member of the gang," Joe said, "and I never had a nickname."

I thought about it. Then I gave a humorless chuckle. "Well," I said, "that ought to clear you, Joe. But it puts me on the hot seat. I never heard those nicknames until last night."

"What does that have to do with it?" Haywood asked.

"I'd be more likely to get one wrong."

Joe nodded. "Yes, whoever thought I was called 'Tater' obviously wasn't a member of the Sharks. Or anybody who was close to them."

Joe sat back and folded his arms across his chest. His eyes narrowed slightly. To me, he looked slightly defiant. *Hmmm.*

Joe spoke again. "And the writing doesn't tell you anything. It's just printing. And anybody could have notebook paper like that. Also, it's written with what looks like an ordinary lead pencil."

"Hmmm." Haywood gave a disgusted snort. "I'll toss it on to the lab guys, but I guess that note's not going to be any help."

"It could be some," Joe said. "It tells you the killer didn't go to WPHS—at least at the same time Spud Dirk did."

"Or that he doesn't want us to *think* he did."

"Where did you find it?" Joe threw the question out casually, but Haywood ignored it.

Instead, he got down to business. Had we seen anything? A strange car? Anyone on foot? Flashlights? Had we heard anything odd during the past forty-eight hours? Cars? Voices? Gunshots?

Neither of us could think of anything.

I asked a few questions in return. Had Dirk been shot? How long did they think he'd been dead? Were there any tire tracks? Foot tracks?

Haywood stared at me, but he didn't answer.

Finally I asked, "Can you at least tell me how Spud Dirk was killed?"

"Sure. That'll be on the news this afternoon."

"Well, what happened? And when?"

"When? A couple of days ago. Blunt instrument. Somebody hit him in the back of the head."

Somehow that information was the most chilling yet. In one way, I was extremely relieved. Spud had not been killed by a pistol. Not the one Digger and I found. Nor any other pistol.

Whew!

In another way, a blunt instrument may be the scariest murder weapon of all. While Joe and I had been going about our business—watching television or getting our pajamas on or thinking about what to wear to work—someone had killed a man within a few hundred feet of us, and he had probably used some ordinary object. A rock, maybe. Or a stick. Or a wrench or a heavy skillet or a table lamp.

I shook all over.

Chocolate Lore

Chocoholic Health Terms

Chocolate has, thankfully, joined the list of substances credited with promoting health. We've been urged to drink green tea and red wine and to eat certain vegetables if we want to get healthy. Well, here's just a partial list of terms describing chemicals in chocolate that can offer health benefits.

- Flavanols and Flavonols. Plant compounds that have antioxidant effects and may lower the risk of developing heart disease, some forms of cancer, and diabetes.

- Flavonoids. Disease fighters that can help fight viruses, allergies, carcinogens, and inflammation. These may prevent oxidation of LDL cholesterol (that's the bad one).

- Tannins. These are nutrients that may inhibit plaque obstructions that cause heart attacks and strokes.

- Resveratrol. A compound that may have cancer-fighting properties. It may also help fight heart disease.

(*The Healing Powers of Chocolate* by Cal Orey)

Chapter 6

Joe quickly put his arm around me, and after a few seconds I stopped shaking. Or maybe I didn't. It was a pretty trembly situation.

Hogan and Hal left after that episode. Soon most of the crowd at the Bailey house cleared, although when I looked down the road I could see yellow crime scene tape draped across the bushes and a patrol car in front of the house. So the investigators were likely to be back.

In the meantime, I tried to keep busy with the material on the Showboat Theater that Maggie had given me. She had scheduled a planning session with her committee that afternoon, but it looked as if I were unlikely to make it.

Joe also looked over some paperwork—lawyers never run out of that—but by five o'clock he was sitting on the screened porch again. I went out and asked if he'd like a beer.

"Great idea," he said, "unless we're going out for dinner. I don't want to have a murder next door and get picked up for DUI all in one day."

"Dinner out sounds terrific. If I don't have to get dressed

up." I had dressed for the office previously, but in Warner Pier business wear is pretty informal.

"How about pizza?" Joe said.

"Sounds great. But first, I have a few questions."

"Such as?"

"How have I managed to live in Warner Pier for five years without meeting Spud Dirk? Especially when you knew him all along."

"Oh, I'm sure you've seen him at the post office or the grocery store. But if nobody introduced you, you wouldn't know who he was."

"Who was he?"

"Just a guy I was in high school with. There was nothing very distinctive about Spud." Joe grimaced. "Well, maybe there was. Spud tried hard to be Mr. Personality. He always had a funny remark or a new joke. Or an old joke. But the dull person inside Spud kept peeking out. He worked at being the vivid personality he wasn't. The result—at least to me—was that he always seemed phony. We weren't close friends in high school, and I found him more and more annoying as we got older."

"So he didn't have a very attractive personality?"

"Maybe that was just how he hit me. Lots of people seemed to like him. Actually I think he may have been a candidate for homecoming king in high school, and he seemed popular enough around town more recently. He and I just didn't click."

"How did he get to be one of the Sharks?"

"I don't think they had an official method for picking their members. Maybe he lived next door to one of them when they were all in elementary school. But the main quality they all shared was that they were school leaders—or they thought they were. The Sharks weren't a formal organization, of course. I'm sure they didn't have an initiation or pay dues or hold formal meetings."

"What did Spud look like?"

Joe got up and went to the bookshelf in the corner of the living room. He pulled a yearbook off the bottom shelf and walked back to the porch, flipping the book open as he came. He sat down next to me and put the book in my lap, pointing to a picture in the senior section.

"That's him. Bring back any memories?"

The portrait was fairly large, because seniors get special treatment in small-town yearbooks. I studied it. "Richard 'Spud' Dirk," the caption read. "Most fun-loving."

The photo showed a blond guy with a long, oval head—to be honest, the kind of head that always makes me think of a fish. But Spud didn't have a wide, fish-shaped mouth. No, he had a tight little mouth in a sort of a pout, and rather big eyes. Of course, in the picture he was twenty years younger than the guy found dead in the carport cabinet.

A faint memory stirred. "Did he work for Allied Realtors?" I asked.

"That's right."

"His picture used to be in their ads."

"Right again. Spud was an agent for them until a couple of years ago. When he left he told everybody he was going to try developing a tract of land north of Warner Pier. And you probably know that he owned the old peach orchard."

"'Our' peach orchard?"

"The one on the other side of the Bailey house. Not ours, of course. But the one that Spud wanted to develop. Or use as a site for an addition of cottages."

"The one that made him mad at you—at us?"

"Right. The Bailey house comes with access to the back road, and he would have needed that."

Joe stared into space a moment, then sighed. "Frankly, I don't think he was very successful as a developer. He had developed a rep—a reputation for sharp dealing. Maybe I quit liking him because of that."

"As far as real estate deals went," I said, "where did he get financial backing?"

"I have no idea. Maybe he had been more successful in selling houses than I realized. Or a sharper dealer than I realize."

"Did he have any partners?"

"I didn't hear of any. But a lot of things could have happened to Spud, and I would never have heard anything about them."

"Was he married?"

"A woman named Star. I seem to remember she was from Allegan. I met her, but I don't remember much about her. I guess I only remember her name because it was unusual."

"Which says something, I guess. If you didn't remember her."

"You're probably right. She must not have made a big impression. But I guess that makes sense. Spud would probably have gone for a quiet girl, one who would have given him an audience. He wouldn't have liked someone who would compete with him in the personality department. Anyway, their marriage apparently didn't work, because I'm pretty sure I heard that they were divorced."

"I wonder if he left any property."

"Probably not. I think Spud's development deals were pretty small stuff."

"How about parents? Brothers and sisters?"

"I think he outlived his parents and was an only child."

I stared into space. "So? Who would have a motive?"

"What do you mean?"

"A motive, Joe. Your onetime acquaintance Spud didn't have a wife; he didn't have parents or siblings. He apparently didn't have business associates. That eliminates most of the reasons that anybody would want to kill him. So what was going on? Why is Spud dead? And why on earth was his body found at the Bailey house?"

Joe leaned over and gave me a kiss. "I don't know the answer to any of those questions," he said. "And I don't want to know. And I don't want you to know."

"But—"

"No. Lee, this is Hogan's case. You and I will pretend the Bailey house isn't there until that crime scene tape goes down. And then, as soon as we legally own the property, we begin to tear stuff out of that house. Starting with those cabinets in the carport. Get me?"

"Yes, Joe. You're saying we don't want to be involved."

"There's no reason we should be. And now, please begin thinking about the pizza toppings you want tonight."

"Okay." I sighed. "Pepperoni, mushrooms, and Italian sausage."

"Same old choices? How about pineapple, anchovies, and chocolate?"

"No chocolate. I get enough sweet stuff at home."

Joe chuckled. "Comb your hair and get a jacket, babe. My stomach's nagging me because we never ate lunch."

A half hour later we were at the Dock Street Pizza Place, Warner Pier's contribution to the world of classic pizza, with both of us sitting on one side of a booth.

The Dock Street has no real competitors with pizza fans in our end of west Michigan. It's an old-fashioned place—oilcloth on the tables, 75 percent take-out business, dim lighting, and nothing on the menu but pizza, salad, and bread. Plus sauce that can make you hear the angels flapping overhead. It's fabulous.

And it's a community center. If we don't run into anybody we know at the post office, we're sure to see someone familiar at the Dock Street.

Joe and I had ordered a large pizza with our favorite toppings—he wanted onions, in addition to my choices—and we were finishing off our salads when a woman materialized beside our booth.

I describe her arrival as "materialized" because she managed to walk up without our noticing her. The Dock Street lighting is dim, but not that dim.

I jumped when I saw her standing there; I hadn't had any warning that she was approaching. She seemed to have floated up to the table without even touching the floor.

She wasn't a waitress. They wore jeans and T-shirts embellished with the Dock Street logo, and this person had on black slacks and a heavy sweater. Her hair was blond, with deliberately dark roots. She was thirtyish, and her face was ordinary, with small features.

Who was this? And what did she want?

I was on the inside of the booth, looking toward Joe on the outer side, so I had seen her first. I nudged Joe and nodded toward the new arrival. He looked toward her and gave a startled jump that imitated mine.

"Hi," he said. "It's Star, right?"

"I was afraid you wouldn't remember me." Her voice was almost too soft to be heard.

Joe was struggling to get out of the booth. "I remember. And we're terribly sorry about Spud. I mean, Richard."

"Chief Jones told me this afternoon. I admit it was a shock."

By now Joe was on his feet, and he waved toward me. "This is my wife, Lee."

I scooted over and held out my hand. Star took it, and we looked each other over.

So, this was the ex—the former wife of Spud Dirk, whose body had been found at the house we wanted to flip. She didn't look heartbroken. Solemn, that was the word. Suitably serious, yes, but not ready to break out in sobs.

"Lee," Star said. "From TenHuis Chocolade." She turned toward Joe. "She's awfully pretty."

"I think so." Joe waved toward the seat opposite ours. "Won't you sit down?"

"For a minute." Star sat. "My mom's back at the house. I wanted to get away from her for a little while, so I came to pick up pizza."

An odd thing to say, I thought. But heaven knows that on occasion I've had houseguests I wanted to get away from, so I could understand.

Joe may have wanted me to stay out of the investigation of Spud's death, but that didn't keep him from asking Star some questions.

"I'm sure the detectives have talked to you. Are you worn out?"

"They were polite. And I didn't know anything to tell them.

I hadn't seen Richard since our last session at the lawyer's office. I guess you know that we had split up."

"There aren't too many secrets in a town the size of Warner Pier. Are you still living here?"

"Yes, I have a job at the bank. I can't afford to quit. And I was to get the house, once I got Richard out of it."

Joe nodded. I had the feeling he was running out of questions already. But he went on.

"Is your divorce final?"

"No. I guess I'll have to settle Richard's estate. He was already driving me crazy over the way he was hiding money. That was one of our big problems."

"The estate will depend on how he left things. If he had a will. Lots of legal details."

Star sighed. "I guess I can't just turn my back and walk away."

"I know there are situations when people wish they could do just that. But it eventually catches up with them."

Joe pulled out his billfold, took out a business card, and handed it to Star. "You probably know that I work for an organization that offers free legal assistance."

Star nodded.

"If you need help handling things, come and see us. Even if you decide to hire a different lawyer, we can talk about how the system works, how to find an attorney. You won't be committed to anything."

"Thanks. But . . ." Star frowned.

Joe sat quietly, waiting until she went on.

"It's just that . . . Well, I'd hate to take your time if I decide to sue you."

Chapter 7

I'm sure my chin hit the table kerplunk. I was totally surprised.

Even Joe, who has a lawyer's skill at keeping his face unreadable when he wants to, blinked and raised his eyebrows. Star was the only one who kept expressionless.

Joe regained his professional deadpan before he spoke to Star. "What grounds would you have for a suit?"

"Richard told me he had a letter granting him the right of first refusal on the Bailey place."

"If so, he hadn't come forward with it," Joe said. "Hogan and I are having our lawyer look everything over, of course. It appears to be a perfectly ordinary sale."

Star was deadpan, too. "You know Richard. Always on the make."

"Then I'm surprised he hadn't come forward with a claim."

"He may have been waiting until you and Chief Jones had put actual money into the project."

"Have you found the letter?"

"I haven't tried to look for it yet."

"I'd advise you to consult a lawyer before you say too much."

Star shrugged. "I'm not much of a fan of lawyers."

"Maybe not, but sometimes—"

Another figure loomed up right in the middle of Joe's reply. "Here's your pizza, Mrs. Dirk," the figure said.

This time it was one of the waitresses. Star slid out of the booth, stood up, and took the pizza box from her.

She spoke over her shoulder as she headed for the door. "Nice seein' you guys." And she was gone as inconspicuously as she had come.

Joe and I stared after her.

I spoke. "Was that for real? Could she cause trouble with the sale of the Bailey house?"

"Not very likely," Joe said. He thought a few seconds. "Though from the gossip I heard, that might have been the kind of stunt Spud would have pulled. Complicating the sale with a last-minute hitch. Anyway, let's forget it for now."

We did. And the pizza was delicious. But thoughts of legal problems with the Bailey house flitted through my mind like mosquitoes on a hot summer night. And they were as hard to chase away as the mosquitoes would have been.

Darn Spud, anyway, I thought. *He may cause even more trouble dead than he would have alive.*

Joe didn't say much more, but as soon as we were home, he called Hogan and told him about Star's claim. They discussed it for at least twenty minutes. Finally Joe sighed.

"It will probably come to nothing, Hogan. I'm sure Twyla and Tad hadn't made any such agreement. And if Mr. Bailey made such a deal with Spud, and Spud wanted the house, I can't think of any reason Spud wouldn't have brought this up back when he was angry about our buying the property. Most letters like that would end the right of first refusal with the death of Mr. Bailey. It's unusual to extend that right to the heirs. So Spud's logical action would have been to bring the whole thing up when sale negotiations first began. Any other action doesn't make sense.

"Tomorrow I'll dig out the law books and see if there's an angle I've forgotten. And there may be. Real estate isn't my specialty."

"Have you reached Twyla Bailey?"

"No, she hasn't called back. I'll call her again as soon as I hang up."

But when he tried Twyla McDonald's number, she didn't answer her phone.

"I wish I had a cell number for her," Joe said.

"How about her brother?"

"He left the sale entirely up to her."

"But he may know how to reach her. Do you have his number?"

"I have some number in Oklahoma. Dadgum! He's a soldier, after all. He's likely to be in Afghanistan or somewhere. That's probably why he had his sister handle the sale."

"The sister was the only one who came for the funeral, as I recall."

"You're right. Tad wasn't here."

Joe dug through his file on the house purchase, and after a moment he held up a letter and waved it triumphantly. "Found it! Tad Bailey's number. On a letter authorizing his sister to sell the house."

"Now to hope it works."

"Cross all your fingers. I'll put the phone on speaker."

Luck was with us. Tad answered on the second ring. When he heard who was calling, his voice became filled with disbelief.

"Joe Woodyard? From Warner Pier?"

"That's the guy. A voice from your past."

"And luckily one I don't mind hearing. What are you up to, Joe? Don't tell me you're organizing a class reunion!"

"Not that! Did Twyla tell you my wife's uncle and I are buying your folks' house?"

"That's great news. But, no, I hadn't heard it. I've been out of the country, and I haven't tried to call Twyla since I got back. How much is she soaking you for?"

Tad laughed after Joe stated the price. "I'm afraid you're getting took."

"You should have paid some attention to the old hometown, guy. Things have changed."

"Hard to believe."

"Tad, you know that my wife and I live in the old TenHuis house now?"

"Yes, my mom was thrilled that it stayed in the TenHuis family."

"Getting it was a big windfall for us. People are probably accusing me of marrying Lee for her real estate."

"You're kidding. That's a pretty farmhouse, but I wouldn't have thought it was particularly valuable."

"Anything with 'Lake Shore' in its address is now valuable. And, Tad, that includes your folks' house."

Tad whistled. "I'm glad Twyla knew that. She always had the best business head in the family. And she went back to see our folks now and then. I always made them come to see me."

Why was that? I gave a fleeting thought to the oddities of family interactions, but I didn't interrupt the conversation.

Tad went on speaking. "Anyway, I left the whole deal to Twyla."

"Yes, but I need to talk to her, Tad. And she's not answering her home phone. Do you have a cell number for her?"

"Sure, but I'll have to find it. It's in my cell phone, and I'm one of those guys who can never remember where I left that gadget."

"That's better than being one of those guys who glues it to his ear. Do you want me to call back?"

"Oh, my wife is bringing the phone to me. But why do you need Twyla? Is there a problem with the sale?"

"I hope not." Joe gave a quick outline of the recent events, beginning with the discovery of the pistol in the basement.

Tad's reaction was amazement. "Good night! I never knew of my parents having a gun in the house. I have no explanation for that."

Joe asked several more questions, then went on. "But you haven't heard about the most exciting thing that's happened," he said. He went on with Hogan and me finding Spud's body.

Again, Tad claimed complete surprise. "You have got to be kidding! Spud? I sure was mad enough to murder him a couple of times when we were growing up, but luckily, I never acted on the impulse. This just seems impossible."

Joe ended his tale with Star's claim that Spud might have had a legal claim that could hold up the sale.

That seemed to me to be a pretty interesting story, the type that can call forth comments such as "Oh my goodness!" or

"Mercy me!" or even a stronger response. But Tad listened to the last part without comment.

When he spoke again, his voice had become cold. "Listen, Joe," he said. "I'll call Twyla and then I'll get back to you."

"Can you give me her cell number?"

"I'll wait until I talk to her. If I'd known that that rat Spud Dirk was mixed up in the deal . . ."

"I didn't know you had a problem with Spud. After all, you were both Sharks."

"Yeah. He was a great white, and I was a hammerhead." Tad sighed. "I'll get back to you."

"Tad! What's the problem?"

"If you want to know, try asking the other Sharks," he said. Then the line went dead.

Joe and I stared at each other. I shook my head. "Honestly, Joe! Tonight every conversation seems to be full of surprises. If my jaw hits the table one more time, I'll probably break a tooth."

"We do seem to be getting unexpected reactions." He reached for his cell phone and thumbed the Google app open.

"Joe? What are you doing?"

"I'm looking for phone numbers. If Tad thinks the Sharks could help, I'll try to find them."

The problem with asking the Sharks anything, of course, was that three of the five left town as soon as they graduated from high school. Spud Dirk and Brad Davis had been the only two who stayed in Warner Pier. We'd already talked to Tad Bailey, and it might be hard to get hold of Sharpy Brock and Chip Brown.

"I guess you can ask Digger where his brother is," I said.

"Yes, I could do that. And I may have to. But Digger's a gossip. I'll try to find Chip without going through Digger. If I talk to him, by tomorrow it'll be all over town that I'm calling him at the request of Hogan."

"You said Sharpy was teaching in college somewhere. Does he have any relatives here who might have an address?"

"I don't know. I could just ask my mom. Or I might be able to find him on Google. If I remember his first name."

"Right. I doubt there's a Dr. Sharpy Brock at any college."

"I seem to remember that his first name was James." In a minute Joe gave a satisfied "Ah." Then he looked at his watch. "Eight o'clock. That's not too late to call."

"It shouldn't be. Where is he?"

"Missouri. It's an hour earlier there." Joe reached for the phone. Almost immediately he was leaving a message. "Hi, Sharpy. I mean, Jim. It's Joe Woodyard, a voice from your youth. Please call me back."

He added his cell phone number, then hung up and reached for the yearbook. "Good luck with that. Now if I can find Chip's real name, maybe I can try him. He was called Chip even in elementary school."

Chip's real name was Yonker C. Brown Jr., the yearbook revealed. No wonder he went by "Chip." But it was lucky for us. With an unusual first initial to look for, an address and phone number in a suburb of Detroit came up immediately.

Unfortunately, when Joe called the number, nobody but a machine answered. Joe left a number and hung up.

"Stymied," Joe said. "I'm beginning to think it's some special psychological effect stemming from Spud."

"What do you mean?"

"I mean that even from beyond the grave Spud doesn't want us to talk about him, so some sort of mystical vibes are blocking information."

I laughed. "Joe, I'm going to draw the line at being haunted."

"Ordinarily, I would feel that way, too. But we're sure blocked from getting information about Spud tonight."

"I refuse to blame the occult."

Joe shook his head. "I'll try to call Brad Davis. Maybe he's not in touch with the beyond the way we seem to be."

Chapter 8

Brad's private number, we found, wasn't available in any of the three phone books that cover Warner Pier. Joe also couldn't find it online, even though we both knew where the Davis family compound was located. It wasn't more than a mile from us, in a more upscale area along Lake Shore Drive.

"We know where he lives," I said. "I suppose we could go to the gate and raise a ruckus."

"And have the security system alarm bells going off? I guess I'll wait until morning and try his office."

We both avoided any conversation about Spud Dirk for the rest of the evening. But I knew Joe hadn't forgotten. I could tell by the way he didn't mention words such as "flip," "loan," "mortgage," or "property." Their absence was significant.

Joe wasn't one to dodge a problem for very long. When I brought the coffeepot to the table at seven thirty the next morning, he was already looking up the number of the VanHorn-Davis Foundation.

"It's pretty early to be calling a business office," I said. "I was going to wait until nine o'clock before I called to ask about getting a set of guidelines on how to apply for a grant from the VHD."

"I can always leave a message," Joe said. "But I want to reach Brad as soon as he's available."

He had to leave a message, but he left it with a person, not a machine. And Bradley Davis replied before Joe left for his office in Holland.

Their greetings weren't as complicated as the greeting with Tad had been. Since Joe and Brad lived in the same town, the "What are you up to these days?" question didn't arise. But this was a touchier situation. I waited to see how Joe would approach it.

Naturally, he tackled it head-on. "Brad, had you seen much of Spud Dirk recently?"

There was a brief silence before Brad answered. Then he laughed. "I saw as little of him as possible," he said.

"So you weren't part of the Spud Dirk fan club?"

"We didn't quarrel in public . . ."

"You mean like he and I did."

"The way I heard it at the coffee shop, Spud didn't give you much of an out when it came to quarrelling. But how can I help you?"

"Have you heard what happened to Spud?"

"I heard he'd been killed. But I don't quite believe all the supposed details that are flying around town. Do you have the real story?"

"As much as is known, I guess."

I was relieved when Joe managed not to mention the pistol Digger and I found. Since Spud hadn't been shot, I was assuring myself that his demise had nothing to do with that.

No, Joe's story ended with our meeting with Star in the Dock Street Pizza Place.

"Star's claim leaves me highly curious," Joe said. "Did Spud leave a legal document that could cause Hogan and me trouble with the purchase of the Bailey house? Or was Star simply blowing off steam?"

"I've got a question, too, Joe. Why are you asking me?"

"Because Tad told us he thought other Sharks might know something about the way Spud ran his business."

"I certainly don't know anything about Spud's dealings. None of them were with the Foundation. I think Spud had only one connection to the Foundation, and that was that he got a scholarship from us nearly twenty years ago. We are not interested in real estate development."

"Yes," Joe said. "I think most people around here know the foundation only handles charitable and community development grants."

The comments were interesting. Somehow Brad pronounced the word "foundation" so that it started with a capital letter. When Joe said the word, it came out as a more generic term. I expected Brad to tell Joe he was saying it wrong. But all Brad said was, "Correct."

Joe went on. "Of course, I understand that you have a certain number of personal investments."

"True, Joe. But I limit those to publicly traded stocks and bonds. I don't do anything local. You can understand why."

"Sure. You don't want any conflict-of-interest problems with the foundation. I think you're wise. So that's why I was surprised by Star's claim that members of the old Sharks club . . ."

Brad laughed. "Not 'club,' Joe. 'Gang.' For some crazy reason I don't remember, we prided ourselves on being a 'gang.'"

Joe laughed, too. "We're all crazy when we're teenagers, Brad. Which leads me to another question. What broke up the old gang?"

"Broke it up?"

"Yes. I talked to Tad last night, and his reaction surprised me."

"Why was that?"

"He refused to talk about Spud at all. Nothing good. Nothing bad. He just refused to say anything. He didn't even say as much as 'Sorry to hear about Spud.'"

"Interesting."

"So, I thought I might as well try talking to you and Sharpy to find out if your reactions were the same."

This time Brad chuckled. "It does seem weird, Joe. And I have to tell you I don't have anything much to say about Spud either."

"So you're not going to reveal why guys who were supposedly Spud's high school friends seem to be down on him?"

"If there was a reason—well, I guess we finally caught on to what a jerk he was."

"What kind of a jerk was he?"

"Highly personable. You knew him. Outgoing. Always telling jokes. But we began to realize they were usually cruel jokes. The rest of us, we may have been dumb teenagers, but we weren't usually cruel."

I felt surprised. After all, Brad had been the butt of the cruelest joke of all, the fake holdup. But Joe didn't point that out.

"Was there one joke that, well, broke the camel's back?"

"No, the breaking point came as you'd expect it to with guys that age. Over a girl."

"Oh? Anybody I know?"

"I doubt it. This girl was from Allegan."

"Star?"

"Oh no. Not her. I'm not even sure I can remember this girl's name. But both Tad and Chip liked her, and she was playing them against each other. But they were friendly about it. Then Spud got in the act. Swept her off her feet some way and beat out both Tad and Chip."

"Hmm. That surprises me."

"I recall being surprised myself. At the time. But the result was that Chip and Tad were furious with Spud. Neither of them wanted to pal around with him anymore. Basically, it ended the Sharks."

"Ended them?"

"I'm afraid so, Joe. Listen, I've got a call on another line, and it's one I'd better take. If you have any more questions, don't hesitate to call back. But I don't know anything about Spud and his business dealings."

Brad hung up.

Joe was still frowning at the phone. He reached slowly across and tapped the disconnect button on the cell phone. Then he spoke.

"Liar," he said.

Chapter 9

"Liar?" I repeated the word with a question mark.

"Yep. Tad refused to talk. He said nothing. Brad talked. He gave me a believable story. About a girl making trouble. But I don't think it's true."

"Why do you think he would lie?"

"Do you mean what was his reason for lying? Or what was my reason for thinking he did?"

"Both, Joe." We stared at each other, then I spoke again. "My first question is, what makes you think he was lying? And second, what would be his motive for doing it?"

Joe looked at his watch. "The answers to those questions are too long. I gotta go."

And the louse left. He picked up his briefcase and his suit jacket, gave me a kiss, and was out the door. My anguished cries of "Joe! Joe!" didn't make any difference.

He just hollered over his shoulder, "We'll talk tonight!" And he left.

I was protesting till the end. As his car disappeared down the drive, I even tried calling his cell phone. After all, he made that half-hour drive into Holland, capital of Michigan's Dutch country, three or four or five days a week, so he knew every inch of the road. And he had a phone he could use without holding it to his ear. He could talk to me while he drove. That's not illegal in Michigan.

But the phone was turned off. He didn't answer.

"Dadgum him anyway!" I hung up angrily and resisted the urge to throw the breakfast dishes into the sink from across the room. I didn't really want them to be smashed, but I sure felt like throwing something.

Twenty minutes later I was leaving for the office, ready to deal with the world of chocolate once again. I was still mad, but I had calmed down enough to pretend I wasn't.

Or I pretended until I backed out into our narrow lane, turned toward Lake Shore Drive, and found my van nose to nose with a truck. It was a dirty white truck with a ladder on the back and a guy in overalls at the driver's wheel.

"Drat," I said. Or something like that.

Both vehicles stopped abruptly, throwing up sand. Both drivers put our heads out the windows. We yelled in unison.

"Digger?"

"Lee? I've got something for you!" Digger left his motor running while he opened his door and got out. He walked toward me, waving a handful of papers.

"Can you give these to Joe?"

"What's this?"

"The estimate he wanted."

"Oh." I took the papers. Should I tell him our deal on the house might be coming unraveled?

"Digger, a problem has arisen."

"Yah." Digger was also a native of west Michigan. "I guess so. A dead body." He put his elbow on my open window and leaned toward me. "You think Spud was lying there while we were looking around the other day?"

I shuddered. He had put into words the fear I'd had since Hogan and I found Spud's body in the carport cupboard.

"I don't want to think about it," I said.

"I don't either, I guess. What were you and the chief doing over there anyway?"

"He heard that you and I found a gun, and he wanted to see where it had been."

Digger's face showed surprise. "I didn't hear that Spud was shot!"

"He wasn't. Blunt instrument. Hogan thinks the pistol is a separate situation. Probably no crime is involved." I decided I didn't want to talk about Spud or the pistol or anything to do with the Bailey house. I gestured with the papers. "Do I need to tell Joe anything about these?"

"Nah. It's all in there. It would be a pretty straightforward project." Digger backed away from my window. "Nothin' to it. If you get the house."

Digger went back to his truck and backed down our lane and out onto Lake Shore Drive. I followed, giving him plenty of room.

I had turned onto Lake Shore Drive before I caught onto that "if."

"If you get the house," Digger had said. Why had he said "if"?

The farther I drove, the more that question bugged me. "If." Darn Digger anyway! I hadn't told him that a possible problem over the purchase of the Bailey house had come up. I had started to tell him there might be a snag. But he had cut me off with one of his nosy questions before I got that information out.

So why had he said "if"?

I got to the shop and made my way into my office, still wondering. I guess I brushed off everyone I passed on the way. For one thing, I knew they were going to want to hear about finding Spud's body, and I didn't want to talk about it. So I went to my desk, sat down, opened my computer, and stared at the screen. The other people in the shop—the ones I didn't want to talk to—couldn't tell I wasn't seeing the screen. I was merely staring in its direction.

But I knew this charade wasn't going to last long. Even on an off-season day, with few tourists and other casual customers coming into the shop, TenHuis Chocolade stayed busy. It was October, and we had twenty-plus ladies making bonbons, truffles, and molded chocolates for the Christmas rush.

Halloween is, of course, a major holiday in the world of chocolate. But our big push to design, produce, and ship chocolate for scary-time had come at least two months earlier. Neiman Marcus and other sellers of fancy chocolates wanted their ghosts and goblins safely in storage by the first week of September.

This month TenHuis Chocolade was focusing on finishing up summer's emphasis on truffles and bonbons accented by sea salt, such as champagne truffles, described as "a dark chocolate ganache flavored with liqueur and a smidgen of sea salt, then enrobed with white chocolate and decorated with dark chocolate stripes."

That realization made my mouth water. I reached into my

top drawer and pulled out a small chocolate square flavored with peppermint. And sea salt. Nibbling that recalled me to real life.

I needed to concentrate on business. The phone would ring, the door would open; I couldn't just sit there in my dream world.

So, when the door did open, I took a deep breath, ready to face the world. And the world came in, in the form of a handsome older gent.

He seemed familiar, but I couldn't recall meeting him. I would have guessed him to be in his sixties, and he had a beautiful head of white hair. He was slim, and he wore a classy polo shirt and khakis with a well-tailored tweed jacket. His boat shoes were Warner Pier casual, but they were not a cheap brand. He wasn't young, but he was good-looking and self-assured. In fact, he seemed almost too self-assured. Like arrogant.

He was definitely the sort of customer who might want to buy the younger woman in his life a pound or two of champagne truffles.

I left my desk and walked out to the counter. "May I help you?"

He gave me a long look, and I realized that, up close, his eyes didn't match his attractive exterior. No, they were definitely cold. And when he spoke, his voice was hard.

"Are you Lee Woodyard?" He made it sound like an accusation.

But I answered bravely. "Yes."

"I came to thank you for finding my pistol."

I hadn't been expecting that. I simply stood there staring. I guess I'd had so many surprises in the past few days that I was becoming immune.

So, I reacted in typical Lee Woodyard fashion. I said the wrong thing.

"I'm asteroid," I said. "I mean, I'm astonished!"

The handsome man didn't laugh at me, although his eyes remained cold. I admired his self-control. It's hard for strangers to keep their faces straight when Lee gets her tongue truly twisted.

I spoke again before he could say anything else and ruin the impression of complete idiocy I was making. "To be honest, the plumber found the weather. I mean, the weapon! I was only the one it fired at."

He frowned. "You weren't injured?"

"No, it missed me. I was deafened briefly, but I wasn't injured."

I offered my hand, and he took it. "I'm Dr. Drew Davis," he said.

"Oh! You're Brad's father. I know Brad and Felicia, of course. But how did a pistol you own wind up in the basement of the Bailey house?"

"That is a very good question. I've never been in the house in my life. I certainly didn't leave it there."

"Had it been stolen?"

"I hadn't reported it as such. I knew it had—well, disappeared. It was gone from its usual spot in my collection. I thought it had simply been misplaced. But it had found its way to one of those missing-gun lists. I suspect my son reported its disappearance. He would have used my name."

"I'm glad it turned up. But I'm afraid that you won't get it back for a while. Even though it's very unlikely that it has any connection with the death of Richard Dirk . . ."

"None at all!" Dr. Davis's voice was still hard.

"Unless someone hit him with it. I understand he was killed by a blow to the head. But law enforcement is funny about hanging on to things, just in case they later decide they're important."

"The chief has reassured me that I'll get it back soon."

I nodded, determined to be friendly, even if Dr. Davis's eyes were giving me a chill.

I spoke again. "I guess early models of that pistol are quite sought after by collectors," I said. "How did you get the pistol?"

Dr. Davis went into a long story about a fellow collector he met at a gun show, and how he had to dicker for the gun, even though it was a later model. It was the kind of tale I'd heard from all my father's friends, often about cars or horses or other items popular in Texas. But collectors are the same everywhere, I guess.

My mind wandered off to whether or not I should bring Maggie McNutt and her plan to revive the Showboat Theater into the discussion.

Dr. Davis may have sensed my lack of interest in his adventures in collecting, because he cut his story short. "In the end, I got the gun for just a little more than my first offer. And I certainly don't have any idea how it got into the basement of the Baileys'. But I'm glad you and Jacoby Brown weren't hurt when you found it."

"Jacoby? Oh. Joe always calls him Jack. Or Digger."

Dr. Davis raised his eyebrows, turning his expression sardonic. "Yes, Digger is an apt nickname for him, I think." He held out his hand. "At any rate, I appreciate you and Digger finding the pistol after all these years. Though I'll always wonder just how it got into the Baileys' basement."

I offered Dr. Davis a chocolate, and he accepted it. Then we shook hands, and our interview was over. Dr. Davis left. Our talk had been so businesslike I almost expected to find a bill in my mail the next day. I allowed myself to wonder about the effect his demeanor had on his bedside manner.

But as I went back to my desk I pondered his final remark. Dr. Davis had said he would always wonder how the pistol got into the Baileys' basement.

Why? Why would he wonder? I thought it was perfectly obvious how the gun got there. One of the Sharks put it there. And Dr. Davis's son had been one of the Sharks.

After all, the Sharks had used the basement as a clubhouse. Any member of the group had had all the chances in the world to hide the gun there. And especially if the gun had disappeared after the episode of the fake holdup, wouldn't Dr. Davis have asked his son about it?

So, what was the big question? Why did Dr. Davis wonder how on earth it got into the basement? Was he deliberately ignoring his son's friendship with Tad Bailey, not to mention the fake holdup?

Get a hold on yourself, I told myself. *Quit wondering about things you don't really need to know. Do some work. If a Ten-Huis employee turned out as little work as you have during the past few days, you'd fire her.*

Only by threats did I force myself to concentrate on my own work until seven o'clock, when my schedule decreed I could go home. Then I gave a sigh, sent the counter girl out the front door, and made sure she got to her car safely on the dimly lighted street. Then I went out the back to my parking slot in the alley, carefully locking the doors behind myself. As I drove home, I tried not to think about the pistol or about Spud Dirk's body lying for days in the carport of a house a few hundred yards from ours. I even tried not to look in that direction as I pulled into my driveway.

Our house looked warm and welcoming. There were lights on in the kitchen, the dining room, and the living room. Joe always cooked dinner on the nights I had to stay late, and I could see him moving around, maybe setting the table.

It wasn't until I got out of the car that I saw the light shining against the basement windows of the Bailey house.

Chocolate Lore

Chocolate Is Literally Out of This World

Scientists at the University of Hawaii, Manoa, have found elements of chocolate in space.

According to *Chemical & Engineering News*, published by the American Chemical Society, a team of researchers was investigating chemical events in the icy solid phase of space, not the hot gas phase.

This involved replicating mixtures found in space in a stainless steel chamber, sealing it in a vacuum, then bombarding it with electrons to imitate cosmic rays. A check of molecules formed included chocolate flavonoids.

Existence of these flavonoids had been considered a possibility earlier, but the 2018 work was more conclusive.

The molecules will be used in research toward modeling the early universe.

(Contributed by mystery reader Nancy Peters, who I'm sure understands it much better than I do.)

Chapter 10

I'd barely seen the light when it flickered and died.

For a moment I thought the whole episode was in my imagination. Or had the light been merely an optical illusion of some sort? Maybe a reflection of the lights of a passing car down on Lake Shore Drive?

But as I stood there, questioning my own eyesight, I saw the light again. This time it flickered across the small basement window, then showed up more dimly. And I knew what it was.

A flashlight. Someone was shining a flashlight inside the basement. The person was flashing it around, and the light was bouncing off the walls and hitting the window.

I took a deep breath. Whatever the light was, I couldn't ignore it. It might be nothing—a neighborhood kid, a curious journalist, a nosy neighbor. But I certainly couldn't pretend I hadn't seen it.

But, by golly, I wasn't going over there to check it out unless I had some company.

I picked my way to my own back door as quickly as possible, threw the kitchen door open, and plunged inside.

Joe put his head around the door into the dining room, smiling. He opened his mouth to speak, but I hushed him with a gesture.

"Joe!" I whispered the word, but I still gave it an exclamation point. "I saw a light in the basement of the Baileys' house. From a flashlight. Would the state cops still have somebody over there?"

Joe went on the alert, then whispered back, "I don't think so, Lee."

"Then it's got to be a prowler."

Joe nodded. "I'm sure the state cops are gone. There was no state car sitting in the drive when I came in. And they usually take down the yellow tape and leave the crime scene as soon as the initial investigation is over."

"Should we call the cops? Or go over there and check?"

"Call 9-1-1."

"What if it's one of the detectives? Or somebody else who has a right to be there? Would he or she be inside the house?"

"Beats me. I don't think a legit investigator would be prowling around with a flashlight. He'd probably have a key, and he'd just turn on the lights. We should call in and tell the dispatcher we'd like to know if somebody official is out here."

"If she says no, then I could tell her that somebody unofficial is."

It took about a minute to do that. The dispatcher said she'd check it out. I hung up before she could tell me to stay on the line. I wanted to look at the Bailey house and talk to Joe about it, not be stuck with the dispatcher.

By that time Joe had doused the dining room lights, turned out the fire under something he had cooking, and switched off both the kitchen lights and the outdoor lights. We each grabbed one of the flashlights we keep near the back door for emergencies.

We looked at each other. "I'm going over there," Joe said in a whisper. "You stay here."

"Not on your curiosity bump," I said. I headed out the back door.

As we left, Joe muttered. "Do you have a house key?"

"Yes. My key ring's in my pocket. So's my phone."

I heard the lock on our kitchen door click. At least the bad guy couldn't get in that door while we were out. Or he couldn't get in easily.

We both knew we were doing something stupid, but the two of us moved toward the Bailey house without any further discussion.

We went through the bushes by the path that would be impossible for a stranger to find. Only people who lived there knew why the three round rocks from the beach were arranged into a triangle at the edge of our gravel drive.

The rocks formed a simple arrow that pointed to the almost-overgrown path that ended at the edge of the Baileys' drive. For thirty years the arrow had reflected the neighborly connection between the TenHuis family and the Baileys.

As we walked, I again glimpsed a light through the trees. It flickered on and off, again so close to the ground that I felt sure it was coming from the basement window.

When we came out on the drive of the Bailey house, I could see the bulk of a car sitting there. The artsy design of the Warner Pier Police logo was on the door. The silhouette of a man was behind the wheel. *Whew!* I felt relieved. There was a cop on duty, and he surely knew what was going on.

I knew Joe and I were being silly; we should have stayed at home.

Then Joe called out, and I jumped out of my skin. But the cop in the car didn't react. And the light in the basement went off.

By then I had realized that walking up to a law officer in the dark, without letting him know we were there, was not a good idea. Thank goodness Joe had thought to call out.

But why had the trooper in the car made no response?

Joe was now moving quickly, almost running, toward the parked car. His flashlight was on and the beam bounced as he moved. I followed.

When we got to the car, its driver's side door was slightly ajar. Joe swung it open. Naturally there were no interior lights; lawmen keep those turned off. Joe shone his flashlight into the front seat, and no one was behind the wheel. The car was empty.

I had been mistaken about seeing a cop sitting in the front seat. I'd been looking at the neck rest behind the driver's seat. So where was the driver?

Joe and I both cast light from our flashes around, looking for the missing patrolman. All I saw was a shoe. It was lying on its side, and the beam of my flashlight hit the sole as the light reached the rear of the car.

The shoe moved a few inches.

Joe and I both gasped, and immediately both of us were on our knees beside a still figure stretched out on the driveway's gravel.

It was Jerry Cherry, a Warner Pier cop.

Joe felt his wrist, and I got on my phone, again calling 9-1-1. "Help!" I said. I gave the address of the Bailey house. "We just discovered a Warner Pier patrolman lying in the driveway behind his car. He's unconscious!"

"He needs medical help right now!" Joe said.

"My husband says he needs medical help right now!" I said. "I called earlier because we saw lights in the house."

"I already sent a car to that address," the dispatcher said. "Don't hang up. They're on their way. I'll send an ambulance as well."

How she managed to sound calm, I don't know. I certainly didn't.

Then I heard a creaking noise. It sounded like the noise I'd expect to hear coming from a weird haunted house in a horror movie. "Creak!" it went. "Creak!" The sound was followed by a sudden bang. Then some thuds.

"Stay here!" Joe said. And he disappeared into the darkness. I could see his flashlight, rapidly moving away from me, but that wasn't any comfort.

I wanted to run after him. But what about Jerry? As if answering my concern, Jerry turned over, opened his eyes, and groaned.

That settled it. "Jerry!" I said. "It's Lee! Lie still. The ambulance is on the way. I'll be right back!"

I put my phone in my pocket, jumped to my feet, and took off after Joe, the light from my own flash bouncing around the trees and bushes.

Joe ran to the Bailey house, galloped through the carport, and made a sharp right at the back of the house. A second drive came in there, another gravel road that led to the "back road," the east–west lane that gives access to Lake Shore Drive, which runs north–south.

For a few seconds, three sets of feet were pounding along—crunching over gravel. None of us were running very fast, since gravel simply isn't a solid surface for running. And I was aiming my flashlight at my feet more often than I shone it at the running figures ahead of me. But I got glimpses of Joe, and maybe fifty feet ahead of him I could see a thin figure wearing a light-colored jacket.

Joe yelled, "Stop! Stop!"

But the person in the lead kept running. And one flash of light showed me that he was headed for a car parked on that back drive.

Surely Joe would be able to catch up with him when he slowed down to get into the car.

Then, suddenly, the figure in front halted abruptly and stooped. He stood up, turning to face Joe, and he began to swing his arms around his head. I saw that he was holding some sort of a long stick, and he was waving it in circles like a helicopter's rotor.

"Watch out, Joe!" I screamed.

Fighting his own momentum, Joe skidded to a stop. The stick swung toward him, barely missing his head. Joe ducked, got off-balance, and fell sideways.

The man who had been running wheeled around and ran to the car. He chucked his weapon and jumped inside. Before I could reach Joe, the car's motor started, and the man we'd been chasing took off, headed down the back drive.

I reached Joe and dropped to my knees. "Are you hurt?"

"Only my pride. We'd better get back to Jerry."

We returned to the Warner Pier Police car as quickly as possible, but Joe was limping. He refused to lean on me. In fact, as soon as he found his own flashlight, he sent me on ahead. Although I wasn't sure what I could do for Jerry.

But I went past the back of the Bailey house and through the carport, reaching the drive where Jerry was lying.

Joe called out, "I'll be there in a moment. How's Jerry?"

"He's conscious!"

I knelt beside Jerry and used my flashlight to examine him. He closed his eyes when the light hit his face. That was good. He was breathing. That was good, too. But his breathing was uneven. That was probably not good. A small pool of blood had formed behind his head. Again, not good.

I pulled off my jacket, took the phone and keys from its pockets and stuffed them into my bra. Then I studied Jerry. Would I injure him further if I moved his head and tried to use the jacket as a pad between his cheek and the gravel of the driveway?

Glancing up, I saw Joe's light coming toward me. Or at least I hoped that's what it was. As a former lifeguard, Joe knew a lot more about first aid than I did.

"Joe?"

"I'm coming, Lee."

"Are you all right?"

"Not exactly, but I'm in better shape than Jerry is." He knelt beside me and looked at Jerry.

"I'm afraid to move his head," I said. "He looks awfully uncomfortable."

"Jerry?" Joe said. "Can you stand to lie on the gravel a minute? I think I hear the ambulance."

Jerry groaned. "My head," he said weakly.

"I sure hope that's an ambulance," I said.

"So do I," Joe said. "But I wish I hadn't dropped the ball."

"How did you do that?"

"I didn't get the license plate of that guy's car."

"Oh, the numbers are easy," I said. "Three-three-one."

Joe gave a deep sigh. "You are crazy," he said. "Completely gaga."

"Hey, big boy," I said. "Don't forget you married an accountant. I've never met a number I didn't like."

Joe screwed his face up until he looked like a handsome orangutan. "Yah," he said. "You've got a lot of talents."

Chapter 11

An hour later, Joe and I were in our kitchen when Hogan called from a hospital in Holland. He told us that Jerry Cherry was still groggy, but he was talking, and his talk made sense, if remarks such as "Where am I?" could be called sense.

Jerry had a splitting headache and a number of other symptoms, but the doctors thought he'd be okay in a few days.

Twice Joe assured Hogan that he was still feeling fine and didn't need to go to the ER. His fall, when he ducked to miss the whirling branch, didn't seem to have injured him seriously.

"Yes, Uncle Hogan," he said. Joe only calls Hogan "uncle" when he's being sarcastic. "Yes, I'll be sure to take a hot shower. Yes, I know I'll be stiff tomorrow."

Hogan signed off by saying he had to check one thing out, but then he'd probably be by the house to talk to us. He declined to say what he might want to talk about.

He also didn't say anything about the hunt for the prowler Joe and I had chased at the Bailey house. I gathered the chances of finding the prowler's identity weren't quite as hopeful as either Joe's or Jerry's condition.

Even if I had remembered the license plate numbers correctly—and despite my "I never met a number I didn't like" claim, it was certainly possible that I hadn't done that—having only numbers with no corresponding letters was not a lot of help.

And neither Joe nor I had gotten a good look at the prowler's car. Neither of us could guess at the make or the model. We also couldn't guess at the identity of the man—or it could have been a woman—who had been driving it. We had only a vague sense of the size of the car; it wasn't tiny, and it wasn't a limousine. The color wasn't white or silver or even light blue. It was dark—black, navy, or some similar color. To me it had been a big blob of darkness on a dark road. Joe didn't seem to know more than I did.

The weapon its driver had been waving around had been a tree branch. Apparently the prowler had simply picked it up off the ground and swung it around. After Joe went down on his keister, the intruder tossed the branch aside. The police didn't feel hopeful about finding fingerprints or anything else on it that would help identify the prowler.

I was feeling shaky, but I was so relieved that Jerry seemed to be getting better, that the prowler hadn't hit Joe with the branch, that the guy hadn't had a gun—well, so many bad things that could have happened had not happened that it left me almost giddy. Or maybe it was low blood sugar. By the time the ambulance had taken Jerry away, neither Joe nor I had been hungry. We packed the dinner he'd been cooking—baked beans and ham with frozen spinach—into the refrigerator to eat some other time and began to clean up the kitchen.

After the excitement in the neighborhood—sirens, lots of police cars, even a brief time when roadblocks were set up—several neighbors called to find out what was going on.

Oddly enough, one of the curious neighbors was Dr. Drew Davis. He lived within a mile of us, and he called to find out why he had been stopped by the state police and asked to show ID before he could turn into his own driveway. This had left him rather huffy.

I had answered the phone, but when he asked to speak to Joe, I merely tapped the button that allowed us both to listen.

"Woodyard? Just what is happening?" the doctor asked. "I'm beginning to wonder if this neighborhood is safe for my grandchildren."

"I certainly understand why you would feel that way," I told him. "Believe me, we're not happy about it either. But there was some sort of prowler at the Bailey house, and the police were trying to figure out what was going on."

"Hmm. I certainly hope they catch the culprit quickly."

"Oh, they'll be looking," Joe told him. "A policeman was attacked. Law enforcement takes that sort of thing very seriously."

"We all should take it seriously," Davis said. "To attack an officer of the law. This must be a desperate criminal."

Joe rolled his eyes. He dislikes being lectured. "If you see anything suspicious," he said, "I know the cops would like to hear about it."

He hung up shaking his head, and turned to me. "I'm getting tired of waiting to hear what Hogan wanted to tell us," he said.

"We'll just have to hang in there," I said.

An hour later, coffee was sounding good while we waited for Hogan to come by to talk to us again.

I spooned French roast beans into the grinder and spoke. "Maybe Hogan will say that Jerry can identify the man who attacked him."

"The person? Someone who came up behind him and hit him on the head? I assume this was the same human being I chased and who beat me into the ground with a tree branch. He was right in front of me, but I can't even say if it was a man or a woman. It was just a person in dark pants and a light jacket."

"I saw the culprit, too, and I'm betting it was a man."

Joe grinned. "You're just being sexist. Always blame the man!"

I gave him a kiss, and at that moment the doorbell rang.

I jumped about a foot off the floor, while Joe jumped even higher than I had.

"Can that be Hogan?" I asked.

"I doubt it," Joe said. "He said he'd call when he was on the way."

I grabbed Joe in a bear hug that could have broken a rib. "Oh no! I don't want to see anybody else!"

Joe patted me. "Lee! Lee! It's okay!"

"You don't know that!"

"Maybe not, but the state police said they were leaving two patrol cars here. If Frankenstein is on the front porch, the patrolmen won't let him come to our door."

"The patrolmen were not going to wait here! They're at the Bailey house!"

"Which is just a couple of hundred feet away. Plus, I doubt a bad guy would ring the doorbell. I'll go see who's there. But you'll have to let go of me."

"You let go first!"

"We'll go together."

I managed to pry my arms from around Joe's middle, and he took my hand. The two of us cautiously edged into the living room. When the doorbell rang again, we both jumped once more, but we didn't leap quite so high this time.

Still, when we got to the front door, Joe didn't just fling it open and yell, "Welcome!"

No, he made sure the chain was on, and he opened the door a crack. But his voice sounded calm when he spoke.

"Who is it?"

"It's me! Star!"

Star? The ex-wife of Spud Dirk? The man who'd been killed? What could Star want?

Joe took the chain off and opened the door wider. "Star? What's going on?"

A male voice came out of the darkness. "That's what I want to know."

Star screamed softly, if it's possible to do such a thing. Then she called out, "Who's there?"

"State police," the voice said.

Joe opened the door wider, and Star dived into the living room and hid behind us. She looked terrified.

A uniformed officer stepped onto the porch and faced the front door. "I'm on duty here," he said. "Any problem, Wood-yard? You know this woman?"

"Yes, we know her," Joe said. "The only threat I've ever heard from her was a legal one."

"Okay. You have any problems, flash the porch light. Or yell."

"Thanks," Joe said. He closed the door and put on the chain, then turned to Star.

"What can we do for you?"

Star stood there, shaking and looking around the room. "I just want to know if you guys broke into Richard's house."

Chapter 12

I don't think I reacted to her comment at first. I knew I hadn't broken into anybody's house, and I couldn't figure out what she was talking about.

I guess Joe was as astonished as I was, because he didn't say anything either.

Meanwhile, Star was staring without blinking, turning from Joe to me and back again. She'd gone all out on hair gel, and her short blond hair was standing on end. That added to her frantic appearance.

When I did finally speak, I said something stupid, of course. "Richard who?"

Then I realized she was talking about her almost-ex, and now deceased, husband. She seemed to be the only person who called Spud by his proper name.

I didn't even know where Spud Dirk had lived, but his now ex-wife had come to our door to ask us if we had broken into his house.

Huh?

First, why did she think Joe and I were the burglars? Second, if she thought that, why had she come to accuse us, instead of avoiding us and sending the cops?

After I got through those two questions, I suddenly had an impulse to punch her in the nose. Her idea was highly insulting.

Then I took another look at her face. Yes, "frantic" was the word for it. I didn't know Star well, of course, but she looked as if she needed a little kindness. The woman was rapidly losing it.

I put my hand on her shoulder. "Neither Joe nor I would break into anyone's house, Star. I sure hope you weren't there when the break-in happened. That would be terrier. I mean, terrifying!"

"Oh no! I moved out months ago. But I guess I'll have to settle Richard's estate. I went over there after dinner tonight, just to see what kind of shape the house was in."

Joe was frowning. "Star, Lee and I did not break into Spud's house. But the police are considering Spud a murder victim. They probably searched his house. The search might have left signs that someone had been there."

"They did search. But that was earlier. Yesterday I was over there before they left. The detective told me that they had taken some papers away, but nothing else. I looked around then, and everything looked normal. Not neat. Richard was never neat. But I went back this evening, and it looked as if a cyclone had hit."

"Did you call the police?"

"Oh yes!"

Joe went to the door and clicked the switch beside it, flashing the porch light off and on. In a few seconds the state trooper was standing in the door.

Joe motioned him inside. "Have you heard anything about Spud Dirk's house being burglarized tonight?"

The trooper frowned. "There was a burglary on the radio about half an hour ago. I didn't recognize the address."

"Did you hear anything else about it? Such as, have they arrested anybody?"

"No, nothing about that's been on."

I thought about that.

"Hogan!" I said. "This must be what Hogan was going to tell us." Then I turned to Star. "But what made you think that we might have been the burglars?"

"Who else? Who else would break in and search through things, even the clothes in the closets?"

"But why would Joe or I do that?"

Star sighed deeply and looked at me sadly. "I thought you might be looking for the right of first refusal."

I didn't have an answer to that one. We'd already told Star we didn't have any interest in the right of first refusal. If it existed. Which I doubted.

And since I didn't have an answer, I didn't say anything. It was Joe who did that chore.

"Sorry, Star. We didn't break into Spud's house, and we know nothing about the right of first refusal."

Star looked crushed at our denial. "But what else could the burglar have been looking for?" she asked.

"A right of first refusal normally is just offered by the person who is the current owner of the property in question, the person who would be selling the house," Joe said. "If that person dies, the agreement would simply lose force. It wouldn't pass on to his heirs. If such an agreement was worded in any other way, its legality would have to be settled by the court."

"Oh." Star looked deflated.

"You should check what I've said with your own lawyer. If there's another angle I'm not aware of, we need to hear about it. But at any rate, if there's any doubt, let's let the courts settle it. Okay?"

Star's head drooped. "I was just so angry. I guess I'm not thinking clearly."

"Did you leave Spud's house while the police were still there?"

"They told me to wait in my car. I just took off."

Joe shook his head ruefully. "We'd better let somebody know where you are. The detectives are probably looking for you."

Joe called Hogan's cell phone. Hogan naturally didn't answer, probably since he was tied up investigating a burglary at Spud's house. Duh.

So Joe called the state police, looking for Hal Haywood, since Hal was really in charge of the case. Their dispatcher called his supervisor, and that seemed to get a little more reaction. In a few minutes, Hogan called and told us to try to keep Star there until he could come over.

I finished making coffee, and when Hogan came, we all had some. I put some cappuccino truffles out on a little plate ("almond flavored milk chocolate filling enrobed with milk chocolate and topped with chopped almonds").

Coffee and chocolate didn't make Star's conversation any more logical. She was a nervous wreck, and who could blame her? As she had said herself, she wasn't thinking straight. Hogan's gentle questioning didn't gain any new information. He finally sent her home, this time with instructions to go directly to her own apartment. The Warner Pier Police provided an escort, and Hogan checked to make sure her mother was there at her home waiting for her.

About then I suddenly realized that I was hungry. Hogan also remembered he'd never eaten, so we got out the beans and ham and the spinach, then warmed them in the microwave. The three of us sat down for a belated dinner.

I gave a sigh as I picked up my fork. "This has been one of the craziest evenings I've ever spent."

"It's right up there in the nuttiness running for me, too," Hogan said. "But Joe's the one who took a tumble."

"I'm not hurt," Joe said. "The question is, what do we do next?"

"Did you hear from any more of the old Sharks?"

"Oh, wow!" Joe rolled his eyes. "I dropped the ball there. Hogan, I tried to reach Sharpy and Chip again this morning. Neither of them answered, and then I forgot the whole thing."

"Maybe we can try again after we eat."

"It's getting late," I said.

Hogan grinned. "All the better. They'll understand that we're serious." So we ate our beans, and then while I did the dishes, Hogan and Joe tried calling Sharpy Brock and Chip Brown. Since they kept the phone on speaker, I could hear the conversations.

Joe called Sharpy first, and again, Sharpy didn't answer. But Chip Brown picked up on the first ring. He didn't seem surprised to hear from a high school classmate and the chief of police in his hometown. I concluded he'd already had news from Digger.

After a few routine pleasantries from Joe, Hogan opened by asking where Chip had been and why he hadn't replied to Joe's message asking him to call. Chip assured him he simply hadn't checked his phone.

Then Joe asked a question. "Chip, am I right in guessing Digger called to tell you about all the excitement here in Warner Pier?"

"If you mean Spud getting killed, he did. That's a crazy thing. But, Joe, Chief Jones, I assure you I don't know anything about it."

Hogan spoke. "Had you heard from Spud lately?"

"No. We weren't in regular contact. He was jerk of the year. At least for me."

"How come?"

"Oh, just something stupid. Back in high school I decided I didn't want to fool with him anymore."

"Weren't the Sharks a close-knit group?"

"At one time."

"What happened?"

Chip didn't answer for a long minute, and Hogan didn't say anything either. Then Chip spoke, but he kept his voice cautious. "I could have been wrong. That's why I didn't say a lot."

"Wrong about what?"

"Well. Spud had a sheet of notes—I thought it was a crib sheet. But when I jumped him about it, he said it was only notes. That he had written a few things out about an upcoming exam. But he acted shocked at the idea I would think he would cheat."

Chip sighed deeply, then went on. "I didn't have any proof, one way or another. So I let it go. But the whole thing turned me off on Spud."

"Huh," Hogan said. "I can see that it might." Then he abruptly changed the subject. "You on Facebook? That's one way to keep up on the old hometown."

"Oh, I have an account. But I don't use it to keep up with Spud."

"I guess Digger keeps you up on the hometown gossip."

Chip gave a self-conscious chuckle. "I guess Digger's news is usually more colorful than Spud's."

"So you do follow Spud's Facebook page."

Chip cleared his throat. "It's not Facebook. We just get a sort of newsletter from Spud. I never asked for it. But you know Spud. He started sending a newsletter to all of us, whether we wanted it or not. It's just easier to delete it than to get him to stop sending it. I don't read it regularly."

"But it shows up?"

"Yah. You know how those things work. They get a mailing list going, and you're stuck on it forever."

"How about personal e-mails?"

"Spud's newsletter *is* a personal e-mail. I mean, it's to his clients, businesspeople around Warner Pier and Holland. But he just sends it. I can guarantee nobody ever asks for it!"

"Can you send me a few samples?"

"Probably, if I search my trash file. Believe me, Chief Jones, you're not interested in it."

"I'd still like to take a look at it. Had Spud made any threats or complained of anybody else making some to him?"

"Well, he did say that he and Joe had had a set-to in the post office."

Joe snorted. "Everybody around here already knows about that."

"It was just stupid. His comments, I mean. But that's what was crazy about the newsletter."

"What do you mean?"

"Spud was a Realtor, right? But he hardly ever wrote about selling houses or buying land. His newsletter was more—well, gossipy. I never understood how it helped with making real estate deals."

By the time Hogan left, Joe had agreed to help the investigation by looking over the newsletters that Spud had been sending his old high school friends. Even though I don't think any of us expected that they would provide any helpful information, either about the present or about the past.

But Hogan did get one interesting phone call before he left our house. Of course, Joe and I got only Hogan's side of it.

"Oh, hello, Vic." He stopped and listened, then spoke again. "I can't answer that. You'll have to ask the state police. And I guess his ex-wife will be making funeral arrangements."

Ex-wife. Funeral arrangements. I realized those arrangements had to be for Spud Dirk. Hogan must be talking to Vic VanHorn, from VanHorn Family Funeral Services, the only local company offering such work.

Hogan again paused to listen. "Yes, I've been told there are no immediate relatives. I'll talk to you later, Vic."

I waited for Hogan to hang up, but he was still holding his cell phone to his ear.

"As I understand it, Star is to be his executor. Come on, surely the guy had enough money to bury himself!"

Hogan clicked the cell phone off. "What's the matter with him? He doesn't usually nag me about funeral expenses. That's the family's responsibility."

"I guess leaving an almost-ex-wife to handle things is odd," Joe said. "Vic's probably nervous about her being willing—or able—to lay out the money."

"From what we've heard," Hogan said, "it doesn't sound as if anybody is going to miss Spud Dirk enough even to see him laid away."

Chapter 13

Hogan left a few minutes later. As I got ready for bed that night, I couldn't get his words out of my mind. Nobody was going to miss Spud enough to see him laid away.

Sad. Sad. Sad. His wife had left him, his old friends had no interest in him, his parents and other family members had died.

Joe said Spud had always tried to be the life of the party. But no one seemed to give a darn about his final celebration, his funeral.

After I'd been in bed for an hour, reading, my blue mood intensified. Joe still hadn't joined me. He had said he'd be along "in a few minutes." But when I went back to the dining room, where our computer lived, Joe was still hunched over the keyboard, reading Spud's real estate newsletter.

I couldn't believe it was that fascinating. "Joe, are you still reading Spud's letters?"

"I'm about to quit." He looked up and grinned at me.

"You look as if you're enjoying them. What's the attraction?"

"I'll tell you in the morning." Joe turned the computer off

and stood up, still smiling. "I didn't mean to leave you in there all alone." He gave me a romantic kiss.

"Joe," I said. "You haven't taken a shower."

"Do I smell that bad?"

"No, but you promised Hogan you would take one. He and I are afraid that tomorrow morning you'll be sore from your fall."

"I'll chance it." Holding my hand, Joe led me around the living room, turning out the lights. "I'm feeling pretty limber tonight."

He did prove himself limber, but Hogan was right, too. The next morning Joe was sore all over and could barely get out of bed. I tried to sound sympathetic, but it was hard. He'd been warned.

"I'm afraid you shouldn't have gone to bed without a good, hot shower," I said. "It might have kept you moving today."

"I'll try one this morning," he said. "Plus a couple of Tylenol."

By the time he got to the breakfast table, he seemed to feel better, whether it was the hot shower or the Tylenol, but I was a little surprised when, even before his bacon and eggs, he called Hogan.

And he gave Hogan a special request. "Please come by as soon as possible.

"I've been mulling over Spud's letters," Joe said, "and I think you may find something interesting in them."

So an hour later the two guys, with a cup of coffee for each and with me as an onlooker, were going over a set of dull sales letters.

"As per your request," he told Hogan, "Chip sent copies of

the letters as soon as he hung up last night. Chip's the way I am about killing old stuff—he procrastinates. He had a dozen of them in his deleted folder. And when I read all of them—and I read them each three times—I saw that they were not actually sales letters."

"What were they?"

"Each of them contained some sort of reference to high school in general, to good old Warner Pier High, to high school pranks or tricks, to Warner Pier in general, even to the history of our area. If Spud told one of his stupid old jokes, he would localize it in some way. And I mean, localize it to be a reference to the old Sharks."

"That's a really odd sales letter."

"Exactly! Maybe if you read one letter per month, they wouldn't seem so peculiar. But when you read a dozen as a group, you see it clearly: these were not business newsletters. So, I went online, found Spud's Web page, and looked at the monthly letters he posted there.

"Now those were typical newsletters, the kind they probably teach people to write in real estate classes. But the letters the Sharks got were different."

"You think Spud was writing special letters to his old high school gang?"

"I feel certain he was, Hogan. Look at this one." Joe punched keys on his laptop, then pointed to the screen. "Spud wrote, 'We'll never forget our unofficial mayor. Sure as shootin' he was a real character.'"

"And another one talks about someone with a 'frozen' personality."

Hogan was frowning. "What could that mean? To anybody?"

"It might be a reference to that local political figure, the one who died the same night as the fake robbery at the convenience store."

"Curley McWhirley? Did he have anything to do with the robbery?"

"Not that I ever heard of. But it doesn't seem like a coincidence."

Hogan didn't look convinced. Frankly, I didn't get the references either.

But Joe pressed on. "The guy's first name was Meyer, Hogan. And the only casualty of the fake holdup was the Frozen Rainbow machine. And that machine sure as shootin' got shot. I definitely think that Spud was referring to that prank."

"But why? You say it was only a joke, and I've talked to a couple of other people, and they agree—everyone says it was just what you say. A prank. A dumb stunt."

"Maybe so. But why did Spud bring it up? It had nothing to do with Meyer McWhirley's death."

Hogan frowned. "Hmm. I guess I'd better pull out the files on that death. If there are any."

After that conversation, it was a downer when we all got up from the computer and went to our jobs. It seemed as if we should be charging up the Warner Pier equivalent of San Juan Hill, rather than asking Hogan to look through some old records. Action seemed to be called for, but only Hogan had anything to do.

I went to my office, but even the Christmas rush at a chocolate company didn't cause my heart to flutter. Until I got an order for a thousand reindeer for Neiman Marcus. Some were to be miniature, some six or eight inches long. Some would have antlers, and some were to pull sleighs. The reindeer were to be in three sizes, with the biggest ones wearing harnesses.

When I added up how much Neiman's would be paying for these, I felt pretty excited. I danced through the new, big commercial kitchen, yelling, "Merry Christmas to all!"

But I heard nothing from either Hogan or Joe until three o'clock, when Hogan called.

"Hey, Lee. I need a favor."

"I owe you a bunch of them. What can I do?"

"I'm going to see McWhirley's widow. She's called a couple of times, asking to speak to me. She seems kind of odd. Any chance you could go with me?"

"Probably. When did you want to go?"

"Right now. I'm out front in the car."

"Well, okay. I'll tell the boss."

"Fine, but don't tell Nettie where we're going."

"Top secret, huh?"

"I doubt it. Before dinnertime, everybody in the county will know I've been out there. There are no secrets in Warner Pier. But I try to be discreet."

I put on my jacket and detoured through the kitchen to tell Aunt Nettie I was going out for a while. I did stop to grab a one-pound box of truffles before I went out the front door. Chocolates make questioning people easier.

As I slid into the front seat of the car with CHIEF on its side, I saw that Hogan was frowning.

"What's the deal?" I asked. "You've questioned thousands of people in your day. Why do you need a chaperone to handle Mrs. McWhirley?"

"It's something about the way she responded when I agreed to come see her."

"What did she say?"

"She sang, Lee! She caroled out a phrase from the 'Hallelujah Chorus.' Then she said, 'Thank the Lord! Maybe someday the mystery of my husband's death will be solved!'"

He looked at me. "And that's a direct quote."

Chapter 14

"But there's no mystery about the death of Meyer McWhirley," I said. "Is there?"

"No one questioned it at the time. Dr. Davis, who was his personal physician, examined the body after McWhirley was found dead on Lake Shore Drive. He said it was a heart attack. Since McWhirley was a heart patient and had been out walking on doctor's orders, nobody questioned it.

"I'm sorry I had to ask you to go along. Mrs. McWhirley's answer sounded a little wacky, and I wanted a witness, preferably a woman."

I laughed. "Well, I am a member of the Warner Pier Police Department Auxiliary."

"Yep. And now you're going to pay your dues."

We both laughed then. The Warner Pier Police Department Auxiliary is a fund-raising organization. We have projects like bake sales to help our small police force buy equipment. It has little to do with law enforcement.

But Mrs. McWhirley's reaction made my curiosity bump throb madly as we drove toward her house. She still lived on

Lake Shore Drive, apparently in the same house where she and her notorious pain-in-the-neck husband had lived at the time he died.

As Hogan turned onto her property, I saw a FOR SALE sign alongside the gravel drive. The name of the listing company was DIRK REALTY. Interesting.

The house itself was a small white frame structure. I guessed that it had been built in the 1940s. Its only eye-catching detail was a trellis at one end of the porch. The trellis was thickly covered with climbing rose bushes, but at that time of the year only a few blooms were still open.

Hogan and I walked up onto the porch, and the door opened before he could knock. A dumpy little woman with curly white hair and pudgy features met us with a smile.

"Do come in, Chief Jones," she said. "I've been wanting to talk with you ever since you became police chief."

"You should always feel free to call me, Mrs. McWhirley," Hogan said. "I try to be accessible to all citizens."

I knew that was Hogan's policy. He was ready to talk to anyone. But he also had a code he could punch on his cell phone, a code that caused the dispatcher to call him and tell him he was needed elsewhere. His patience with the public was limited to about twenty minutes.

Mrs. McWhirley smiled shyly. "Perhaps I should have called earlier, but I received such short shrift from your predecessor that I guess I was procrastinating. I know my husband had become known as a crank, and that city officials were sick of hearing from him. But he was a courageous man, too. If he was convinced that something irregular was going on, he stuck to his guns."

"I'm prepared to listen," Hogan said. "What did you want to report about your husband's death?"

And for the next twenty minutes Mrs. McWhirley retold us the entire story about her husband's death. He had had a heart attack, followed by open-heart surgery. She explained exactly what his physical problems had been and how they were being treated. The nightly walk was part of the prescription. Yes, she had been told that he often stopped and bought a Hershey bar during his excursions, but she had not nagged him about it.

"He was trying," she said. "At least he was trying."

Hogan nodded sympathetically, but I could tell by the way he glanced at his watch that he was thinking he had heard about enough.

Mrs. McWhirley kept talking. "So I wasn't surprised when the list of things he had in his pockets included a large Hershey bar."

Hogan gave another glance at his watch. "But how did you think the Warner Pier Police Department could help you?"

"You mean, after he died?"

Hogan smiled. "Yes. I'm afraid our jurisdiction doesn't extend to what people eat. They're on their own with that."

Mrs. McWhirley beamed. "I know that! And I'm afraid that situation was hopeless. No, I called about the shoes."

"Shoes?"

She nodded happily. "Yes. A pair of white size-eleven walking shoes. Adidas. He definitely had them on when he left the house."

"That sounds logical," Hogan said. "What happened to them?"

"That's what I'm trying to find out! When our neighbor Dr.

Davis found him, he was barefoot! His shoes were gone. He was wearing only socks."

She leaned forward and tapped on the coffee table. "What happened to those shoes?"

His shoes had disappeared? I was as amazed as Mrs. Mc-Whirley was. How could his shoes, well—walk off?

Hogan can take almost any shock without changing his expression, but the news of the missing shoes did make him widen his eyes.

"I agree," he said. "That's very strange. How cool was it that night?"

Mrs. McWhirley gave a derisive hoot. "Too cool to wade in the creek! And I assure you Meyer was not a man who would simply think it was fun to go barefoot. Not along Lake Shore Drive."

Hogan nodded. "You're right. Far too much gravel along the edges."

"I suppose it doesn't really matter in the history of the world," she said. "And it was twenty years ago. It's simply one of those little mysteries. I want an answer. Like my grandfather."

"What happened to your grandfather?" I asked.

"Oh, this was down in Missouri. He was an old farmer. He always slept in his long johns. But this one night he climbed in bed without a stitch. My grandmother was shocked to the core! She argued with him. 'George! George! You can't sleep naked as a baby.' All he answered was, 'Well, I can if I want to. Who's to see?'"

I chuckled. "I guess it was his business."

"Maybe so. Then around two in the morning, Grandpa had

a stroke! He was dead before the ambulance could get there! Grandma was real embarrassed. Then she wondered if there was some reason—you know, something about that stroke coming on made him feel hot."

"Did she ever figure it out?"

Mrs. McWhirley shook her head. "Not that I heard about. But the ambulance men—well, they told her they'd had much stranger cases and not to worry about it."

"That's an interesting story," Hogan said. "But it doesn't explain what happened to Mr. McWhirley's shoes."

He stood up. "Can you show us the exact spot where your husband's body was found?"

"Oh, surely. It was right down at the foot of the drive."

The three of us walked down to Lake Shore Drive. The houses in her neighborhood were not close to the road, so the drive was fairly long. The surface of the drive was small gravel—chat, it's called in some places. Mrs. McWhirley assured us that it was the same type of surface they'd had twenty years earlier, when her husband died.

"Of course, I've had to get it resurfaced a couple of times in the years since Meyer died, but we've always had a gravel drive," she said. "He was found here, right under that big oak tree."

The three of us looked at the spot she indicated. I felt let down. There was nothing to indicate anything dramatic had ever happened there. I wondered if I should say something about the way life goes on. Actually I wanted to shrug.

We walked back up the drive, and Hogan asked Mrs. McWhirley about the potential sale of her house.

"My daughter's been after me to move to Grand Rapids, so

I'd be nearer to her." She gave a deep sigh. "But I don't want to be a burden to her."

"And now you'll have to find a different Realtor," I said.

"Actually I've about decided to stay here for a few years. I think I'll take the house off the market."

"Did you know Richard Dirk well?"

"Spud? Oh yes. His parents lived in the property behind us. He was a nice enough little boy. Maybe on the sneaky side."

"Sneaky?" Hogan sounded interested.

"Oh, nothing serious. If someone came to our house, he'd walk by and check it out. See who it was. His mother was the same way."

That seemed to finish our conversation. Hogan promised to look into the missing shoes, and we left.

"Mrs. McWhirley seems like a nice lady," I said. "But is there any possible way to investigate those missing shoes after twenty years?"

"Probably not."

"What do you think happened to them?"

"Somebody stole them, Lee."

"Really? Stole a pair of shoes off a dead man's feet?"

"She said the shoes were new. Twenty years ago—well, some kid may have been an ambulance attendant and felt that he needed the shoes more than McWhirley did. Or maybe they were simply lost. Somebody at the funeral home may have taken them off the body and laid them aside, and they got put in the wrong box. Or a tramp may have walked by and seen McWhirley before the shoes were missed. He might have desperately needed new shoes. There are lots of possibilities, and—like you said—it was twenty years ago. I doubt we will ever find out."

"So what next?"

"I was going to give the Country Convenience Store the once-over. Do you have time to go with me, or do you need to get back to town right away?"

I laughed. "Hogan, surely you know me well enough to know that fooling around at a crime scene will always be more attractive to me than going back to work."

So we stopped at the Country Convenience Store, the place where the holdup that was not a holdup occurred.

"The Country Store," as it was frequently called in our neighborhood, was fairly typical. It was located near an exit from the interstate. The parking lot would hold maybe a dozen cars. The entrance and exit were fine gravel, like Mrs. McWhirley's driveway, and a concrete pad surrounded the gas pumps and a storage area. Inside, the cashier was not housed in a glass box, but simply stood behind a counter. The store was small and sparsely stocked. Shelves held items drivers or casual shoppers might need. The food section offered potato chips, cheese and crackers, bread, bologna, and a few jars of baby food. Toilet paper, batteries, motor oil, tobacco, and the like were displayed on another shelf. There was a refrigerator with soft drinks, beer, and milk.

I wondered why Dr. Davis would have picked this particular store for his son's first job. Or did Brad Davis find it on his own? But I could certainly see why the Sharks selected it for a mock robbery. At night it would be almost deserted, so their playacting would probably be uninterrupted.

Of course, twenty years ago things might have been different. That was fifteen years before I moved to Warner Pier. Perhaps there was more traffic at the Country Convenience Store in those days. I'd have to ask Joe.

Hogan parked, and we walked in. There was only one clerk on duty, a middle-aged woman. She looked like a typical resident of west Michigan, with straight, light-colored hair and a stocky build.

"Hi, Hilda," Hogan said. "You know Nettie's niece, don't you?"

I'm always amazed at Hogan's ability to pull names out of his mental card file. Though he was in his middle to late fifties when he moved to Warner Pier, he seemed to have met everybody in town.

He explained to Hilda that he was looking into Spud Dirk's death, and he politely asked if he could look around.

"Well, sure," Hilda said. "But Spud sold the place a couple of years ago, you know."

I whirled around to hide the surprise that must have been showing on my face.

Spud had owned the Country Convenience Store?

Chocolate Lore

Chocolate May Cut Hypertension

From a 2018 publication of Harvard T.H. Chan School of Public Health: A study of the Kuna Indians, natives of the Caribbean coast of Panama, hints that high cocoa intake may cut hypertension, or high blood pressure.

The Kuna's traditional diet includes around five cups of cocoa, served as a beverage, every day. Studies have shown that hypertension is unusually low among the Kuna people, even though their salt intake is also rather high.

But when the Kuna move to urban environments, their high blood pressure rates rise. The Kuna who remain on their native islands, however, had higher levels of flavanols and lower death rates from heart disease, cancer, and diabetes than their city-dwelling relatives.

Scientists have long known that flavanols can help protect the heart. They support the production of nitric oxide in the cell linings of blood vessels that help relax those vessels and improve blood flow.

Chapter 15

Hogan didn't turn a hair, but I swallowed my tongue.

Hilda seemed to expect her news would be a shocker, because she waggled her eyebrows up and down and grinned. "Not many people know that," she said.

"I guess not," Hogan said. "Who bought the store from Spud?"

"That's the question, isn't it? Spud never paid much attention to the place—sometimes we even had to wait for our paychecks a couple of days. Then one afternoon he came by and told me he'd sold it. He asked me to continue as manager until the new owner made other arrangements. But no one has ever made any new arrangements, at least any that I'm aware of."

"So who do you report to?"

"Not a soul! I send the time sheets and other paperwork to an investment company. S&J Investments. The bills go directly to them."

Hogan took out his notebook. "What's their address?"

"It's a post office box in Holland. That's all the address I have." Then Hilda nodded enthusiastically. "But they pay salaries on the dot."

Hogan nodded. "Who comes around to check on repairs and such?"

"Nobody!" Hilda leaned over the counter and dropped her voice as if she were going to tell Hogan a big secret. "I could be cheating them left and right. Nobody seems to pay any attention at all to the place. And you see how run-down it's getting? I've written letters to the company, asking what to do about repairs. But I didn't get any reply."

"That leaves you in a bad position."

"Don't I know it! The new people haven't shown any interest, and Spud never even came around to pick up his stuff."

Hogan came close to losing his cool at that. He answered her real fast. "What did he leave here?"

"I don't know, Hogan. It's all in the safe, and I am not authorized to open it."

"Where's the safe?"

"In the office." She led Hogan and me around the counter and into a tiny office. There, on the floor behind a messy desk, was what she had called a safe. It was more of a strongbox, I guess—a heavy metal box with a combination lock. But anybody strong enough to lift it could pick it up and carry it away.

Which is what Hogan did. He loaded it into his car and gave Hilda a receipt. He did ask Hilda if she knew the combination, but neither of us was surprised when she said no.

We weren't out of the store's driveway before I was quizzing Hogan.

"Hogan, what's the significance of the safe?"

"How would I know, Lee?"

"It's not exactly a secure way to keep things. Not like a safety deposit box in a bank."

"Spud didn't have a safety deposit box. At least not around here."

"Oh? So law enforcement knows that?"

Hogan grinned at me. "It would be a routine part of the inquiry, Lee."

"Aw, c'mon, Hogan. You can give me an update."

"My lips are zipped. I'll drop you at your office."

That was the last word I got, so I had plenty of room to allow my imagination to run wild with questions about what Spud kept in his unsafe safe.

Questions such as, why did he leave it at the convenience store, even after he no longer owned the store? And, why did the new owners allow him to do that? And, who were the new owners? Why did they buy the place, then let it become rundown?

These questions were still spinning in my head when Hogan stopped the car in front of TenHuis Chocolade. As I reached for the door handle, Hogan shook a finger at me.

"My lips are zipped," he repeated. "And I hope yours are, too."

I bared my teeth and growled at him. He laughed.

I went to my office and spent an hour snarling at the computer. I was barely polite to my fellow employees. I was simply dying to know what was going on with Spud's safe, and I knew I might never learn.

And when I got tired of that question, there was Mrs. McWhirley's story about the missing shoes. I found it hard to believe that a tramp took them. Or maybe I didn't want it to be that simple.

Grrr again.

I stiffened the old upper lip and reached inside my desk drawer for my private stash of chocolates. I took out a fiery pepper truffle ("dark chocolate center enrobed with dark chocolate, then sprinkled with cayenne and finished off with an accent of sea salt"). The burning pepper flavor matched my mood, and my blistered tongue gave me something different to think about.

For one thing, I calmed down enough to read the messages that had been left for me that afternoon, and the top one was from Maggie. "Can you check on the grant application procedures from VHD? We need to get started on that."

The other two messages didn't seem to need immediate attention. I looked at my watch. Yes, I had time to run down the block to the VanHorn-Davis Foundation before that office closed.

I once again called out to tell Aunt Nettie that I was going out for a minute, but I assured her—and maybe myself—I would stay late to finish my work.

One of the advantages of living in a small town, of course, is that you can get anywhere in the community in a few minutes. I didn't even need to move my van, since the VHD offices were just down the next block, upstairs in one of our antique redbrick business buildings. Those buildings are required to have a historic appearance, thanks to a city ordinance. Practically everything on our major streets is white frame or red brick.

In five minutes I was ringing the bell at the outside door of Brad Davis's office. Over the intercom, a deep voice answered, "Yes?"

"It's Lee Woodyard. Is that you, Brad?"

"Sure, Lee. Come on up. The elevator is at the back of the foyer." He pronounced it "foy-yea." Not "foy-yer."

A foy-yea? The foundation had a foy-yea? Wow!

An electronic tone signaled that the door had been unlocked, and I stepped inside. Wow again. Marble floor in black-and-white squares, shiny chrome facing on the elevator, giant rubber plant. Maybe Maggie and I should apply for a grant to redecorate something.

Since the building was only two stories, I had been surprised by the presence of an elevator. When I got in it, I discovered that the elevator reached three floors—basement, first, and second. Hot stuff. And since the foundation served the handicapped, among others, perhaps the elevator was justified. But I couldn't think of another building in Warner Pier that had an elevator.

I clenched my teeth, swearing I wouldn't tease Brad about his fancy building. I didn't really know him well enough to tease, but when the elevator opened, he greeted me in a cordial manner.

Brad was tall and slender, like his dad, with gray eyes and dark hair. But he didn't have the grumpy-looking facial muscles his father had. Brad always looked a bit cautious to me, while during our brief meeting, his dad seemed to be permanently self-satisfied.

The office was only two rooms: a business office with two desks and a few chairs and an adjoining meeting room. The suite felt spacious because the meeting room had classy furniture and glass walls.

Brad smiled warily as he led me to a chair opposite his desk.

"How do I rate, Lee? A call from Joe yesterday, and a visit from you today."

I quickly explained about Maggie's plan to revitalize the Showboat Theater.

"I've agreed to serve on the organizing committee. Since I'm the one who supposedly has a head for figures, I get the job of begging for money. And grant applications have a reputation for being complicated."

Brad laughed. "You mean that 'you don't get the money because you didn't dot the i on page twenty-nine G?' reputation? We try to keep ours simpler than that. Of course, we are legally required to keep strictly to the rules."

"We're not asking that any rules be broken."

Brad went to a filing cabinet and took out a folder. "Who's on the steering committee?"

"I'd better not say. Maggie has a list, but she hasn't asked them all. I assure you we'll get the required personnel and make sure they're having the required number of meetings."

"And Joe better get out his legal degree, right?"

"I'm afraid he's stuck with another no-fee job. If Maggie can talk him into it."

Brad sat down on his side of the desk, and we went over the grant application. It didn't sound too complicated, but I knew things would come up. Things always do.

Brad was putting all the papers into a big envelope for me when the subject changed.

"And by the way," I said, "you may have been dealing with the Woodyards for the past few days, but I've been dealing with the Davis family."

Brad looked puzzled. "Oh? Felicia?"

"Not just your wife. Your dad. I really appreciated his visit yesterday."

Brad smiled, but he kept stuffing papers into his big envelope. "I didn't know about his visit. Did he have a yen for chocolate?"

"He did eat some when I offered it. But mainly he came by to say thanks to me and to Digger Brown for finding his gun."

Brad stopped moving. He looked at me, but his face screwed itself into a strange grimace. Then it settled into absolute stillness.

"Finding his gun?" he said.

"Yes. The one Digger and I discovered in the basement of the Bailey house turned out to belong to him."

Bradley's expression still didn't change, but the large white envelope he was holding fell into his lap. The papers it held slipped out and flew all over the floor.

Chapter 16

That night Joe and I went to Herrera's, one of Warner Pier's best restaurants. Joe probably wanted to go there because of the food; I wanted to go because it was quick and quiet.

I wanted quick, of course, because I needed to get back to work for a couple of hours. And I wanted quiet because I wanted to discuss Brad Davis and how he'd spilled twenty pages of grant forms all over the floor.

Brad wasn't particularly clumsy. I felt that the accident proved he was upset. Or amazed. Or discombobulated. Or something odd.

Joe scoffed at the idea.

"Honestly, Lee! Anybody can drop something," he said. "You're reading far too much into an accident."

"I wish you'd seen his face, Joe."

"I've never thought Brad was much to look at."

I shook my finger at him. "He was a spectacle this afternoon. His face got—well, crazy. Then it went dead."

"Wouldn't it be more incriminating if he turned pale? Or flushed bright red? Or broke out in purple spots?"

I ignored that comment. "I've known Brad for several years—just casually, of course. But I've always had the feeling that I was only seeing and hearing the top layer of his personality. This time . . . well, it was as if I were finally seeing the real Brad, as if his personality popped out like measles."

Joe grinned. "Again with the spots."

I glared, then we both shut up. I think Joe finally saw that I wanted him to take me seriously. Or he may have realized I was nearing the end of my patience. Anyway, we each tore into our steaks for at least long enough to cut, chew, and swallow a few large bites.

Then I again went on the attack. "There's one thing I'm sure of," I said. "Brad was stunned when I told him the gun Digger and I found had belonged to his dad."

I'd been concentrating on Joe, so I was startled when a deep bass voice boomed in my other ear.

"His dad? Hey, Lee, don't mix it up with Brad's dad. You're likely to lose."

I jumped about three inches off my chair as I turned toward the voice, and I discovered I was facing Tony Herrera, who had been Joe's best friend since kindergarten.

Tony was the son of our mayor, Mike Herrera, who was also Warner Pier's leading restaurateur and a couple of years earlier had married Joe's mom. So Tony and Joe were stepbrothers as well as friends.

As in most small towns, Warner Pier's connections between family and friends look as if a three-year-old drew a diagram of them the first time he got hold of a pencil.

Tony had always tried to dodge restaurant work—for anybody, not just his dad. Even though his wife and two of their teenage children worked in the family businesses, he steered clear and kept saying he would "stick to manual labor."

Actually Tony is a skilled machinist. But at the moment he was wearing a white jacket and holding a big tray, indicating he had been busing tables.

"Oh, Tony!" I said. "What are you doing here anyway? I thought you were merely the father of a table clearer."

"I'm filling in for Alicia. She wanted to go to the football game." Tony frowned. "Some guy on the team has caught her eye. Sorry to be eavesdropping. Even about Brad Davis."

"How did you know what we were talking about?"

"You said 'Brad.' How many Brads are there in Warner Pier?"

Joe waved at an empty chair at our table. "Would the manager get mad at you if you sat down and had a cup of coffee with us?"

Tony grinned. "Nah. She'd probably join us." He moved toward the coffeepot.

Tony's wife, Lindy, manages Herrera's, as well as the Sidewalk Café. She gave us a cheerful wave from behind the cash register.

After Labor Day, when the big crowds of tourists left, all Warner Pier restaurants got pretty informal. Nobody was going to be shocked if Tony stopped busing tables and sat down for a cup of coffee with two of the guests. The tables were all clear at the moment anyway.

Tony likes gossip as well as anybody does. As he stirred his coffee, he looked at me. "I hope you didn't really bump heads with a Davis."

"I hope not, too. I just had a strange experience with one. I guess it only indicated that Brad and his dad don't always see eye to eye. As if it was an unusual occurrence for fathers and sons not to get along."

"It sure wasn't for me and my dad. As you both know. He had me washing dishes beginning when I was fourteen. But working together was miserable for both of us. When I turned seventeen, we gave up trying, and I got a summer job as a lifeguard."

"Yah," Joe said. "Tony and I each spent a couple of summers looking good for the babes at Warner Pier Beach!"

Both of them chuckled. I'm always careful not to ask too much about those days. Now they're both solid family men; then they were harebrained kids. When they talk about "action," I don't think they're always referring to pulling people out of the water.

"I guess it worked," I said. "The first time I saw Joe he was up in that tower. All I could think was 'shoulders!'" We all three laughed.

Then I went on. "And I can understand why a father would like to see his son in a family business. But Dr. Davis apparently didn't want to see Brad as another doctor."

"I think he did at first," Joe said. "I seem to remember Brad complaining about how he hated science, and his dad was making him enroll in Chemistry II."

Tony nodded. "I think that for a long time he wanted to see Brad as a doctor. We used to get together and gripe about being expected to follow in daddy's footsteps."

"What changed it for you and your dad?" I asked.

Tony shrugged. "I don't know exactly. I do remember it was junior year for us, so senior year for Brad. By September the whole situation had changed. The fight was apparently over."

"And both you and Brad won?"

"I did. I convinced my dad that skilled labor was respectable. I don't know how Brad managed."

Joe spoke up. "I seem to remember that it really was quite a change, Tony. Your dad began to be proud of the talents you had understanding how things fit together and of how well you work with your hands. You began to see how hard he had worked to own his own restaurant."

"He had only one restaurant then," Tony said. "And he was proud of it. And, yeah, I was proud of him. But Brad and his dad—it wasn't like they quit arguing about him going to med school. It was more like they quit speaking. Period. Just stopped communicating. I had the impression— Oh, I'd better shut up."

Tony had obviously become uncomfortable with his own remarks. He ducked his head until his nose was nearly in his coffee cup.

Joe's response was a frown. Then he spoke. "You knew Brad better than I did, but I remember that after the Country Convenience Store, the summer of the so-called robbery—" Joe and Tony both grinned at the thought. Maybe I did, too. Then Joe went on. "After that Brad quit working at the store and applied for an after-school job at the bank. I remember he worked real hard on a résumé; he even came by the insurance office and asked my mom to help him with it. And I was under the impression that he managed it all with no strings pulled. No help from his dad."

"That's how I recall it, too," Tony said. "It was like his dad gave up trying to arrange his life, and Brad kind of knuckled down and began to act like a grown-up."

He grinned. "I just hope something like that happens to my kids. Someday."

Two customers left about then, and Tony got up to bus their

table. Joe and I laughed a little, seeing Tony voluntarily doing a restaurant job because his daughter wanted a night off—the same job he had fought with his father to avoid.

We were both refusing dessert when Joe's cell phone rang. I could tell it was Hogan, mostly because Joe's first words were, "Hi, Hogan."

Then he listened. "Okay. We'll drop by," he said.

As he hung up, I groaned. "Joe, I haven't got time to go by and see Hogan. I really do have to get back to work."

"He says he got the box open, and you'll want to see what was in it."

I reached for my jacket. "How quick can we get there?"

Yes, I was really eager to see what was in that box. What had Spud hidden in it? Why had he hidden anything?

The police department was only two blocks away, so we were there immediately. Hogan was watching for us and unlocked the door as we approached.

"Hi, Hogan," I said. "What did you find?"

"Something we all like." Hogan waved his hand at a big table the cops use for paperwork.

And Spud's lockbox was filled with paper, true. Green and white paper. Wrapped in bundles. And each piece of paper had the face of a great American on it. Plus figures. None of them below twenty.

The box held a whole bunch of cash money.

Awe filled Joe's voice as he spoke. "And this was in Spud's office safe?"

"Yep." Hogan's voice sounded serious, too. "Around five thousand dollars."

Chapter 17

Joe and I were still intrigued by the little safe as we walked back to the TenHuis shop a half hour later.

"Money," I said. "We should have known. What else would anybody keep in a strongbox?"

Joe grinned. "I wonder what Spud wanted that money for."

"To hide his finances from Star? She said he'd been tucking money away. That they'd fought about it."

"Did he want to take a faraway vacation?"

"Or put it in his Christmas club!"

"That's as good a guess as any." Joe squeezed my hand. "How long are you going to stay at the office?"

"At least an hour."

"I may go out to the boat shop. I should work on that Peterborough Speedster."

"Maybe that's what Spud wanted the money for! A snazzy boat! He didn't know you don't take cash."

We both laughed, though the subject wasn't really funny. Joe's boat shop specializes in restoration and repairs of antique wooden boats—small ones, such as speedboats or even canoes or rowboats. Hobbyists will pay piles of money to get a 1941 wooden canoe back into mint condition. And Joe charges them piles of money for that service.

And now and then some boat owner hints that if he gets a discount, he can arrange for that pile of money to be paid in cash. The implication is, of course, that Joe can make up the difference by not paying tax on that cash income.

Joe doesn't do this. As a lawyer, of course, he could get in major trouble if such a scheme were discovered, but there are a lot of other possible problems. First, it would put him under the thumb of the cash-only payer. Second, it would infuriate the accountant he's married to. Third, it's just not honest to be a tax dodger, and he's a pretty honest guy.

The latest person to suggest a cash payment happened to be the owner of the 1941 Peterborough Speedster. Joe had replied with his usual bland refusal, saying he didn't give discounts for cash, and the owner had written him a check without more argument.

Could Spud have had some similar scheme in mind? It was, naturally, a possibility, though it was unlikely to involve a boat. He was interested in buying property, wasn't he?

Or the money might even be milked from the operation of a rural convenience store. Of course, leaving his valuables at the store after he sold the property—that would be iffy. Would Spud have been willing to take that chance?

I knew that the state police lab would have gone over the little safe thoroughly, looking for fingerprints or other evidence. Maybe they had found something. Hogan hadn't given us a hint in that direction.

So I told Joe I'd be home in an hour or so, then gave him a

kiss at the door of TenHuis Chocolade. I knew that if he went to his shop, he might get so enthralled with a boat that he wouldn't get home until midnight.

And for the next hour—actually hour and a half—I concentrated on payroll, the money I needed to pay the genius women who make our fabulous chocolates. Only once did I stop. About eight o'clock I ate a mocha truffle ("dark chocolate center flavored with coffee and enrobed in dark chocolate, then embellished with white stripes"). After all, everybody deserves a little after-dinner coffee, right?

I left at nine o'clock, and when I arrived in my own driveway I wasn't surprised to realize that I had beaten Joe home. The outdoor lights had been turned on by our electronic gadgets, but I looked around carefully and gripped a handheld siren as I got out of the car.

Everything looked peaceful at our house. The Bailey house, barely visible through the trees, also looked peaceful. But I hurried through my own back door, remembering the excitement earlier in the week when Spud's body was found.

I put my jacket away, then called Joe. Just because I like to hear his voice, I guess.

He answered on the fourth ring. "How soon are you headed home?" I asked.

"I'll be along in a few minutes."

As I waited, I roamed the living room, looking for the mail. When I found it, I didn't even want to read the junk ads that had been practically the only mail that day. Joe had one personal letter.

So I looked around for something else to entertain myself. And to my surprise, I found one of Joe's high school yearbooks.

The yearbooks usually were on the lowest shelf of the living room bookcase, in a place that was easy to ignore. For a moment I felt surprised to see one on the coffee table. Then I remembered that Joe had pulled it out to show me a picture of Spud Dirk as a high school senior.

I picked the book up and turned it to Joe's class picture. He'd been a junior that year.

Naturally, with twelve to a page, the junior pictures were smaller than the senior pictures. Each senior had been recognized with a quarter-page layout holding a brief story about his or her high school career. Younger students got only names underneath their pictures.

I looked carefully at the picture of Joe at age sixteen. I decided maturity had enhanced his appearance. Even though the sixteen-year-old Joe was good-looking, zits had dotted his cheeks, and he had a passive, slightly shy expression. Today Joe was much more confident.

At least Joe had had a good haircut. Not all the guys could say that twenty years earlier. Hair was longer in those days, but sometimes woolier or stringier or greasier as well.

Next, I checked out Tony Herrera's picture. In those days his hair was short, as in restaurant-worker length, and his eyes were as dark now as they had been when he was sixteen. Tony had had a rebellious look then; in fact, in those days he looked a lot like his own son did now. Each of them had a slightly suspicious frown.

There was still no sign of Joe coming home, so I turned to the senior section. Starting at the top of the list, alphabetically, the first Shark I came across was Tad Bailey. I realized we'd lived next door to each other, in a way, for several years, but I had no idea what he looked like, either now or then. He'd joined the army before I moved to Warner Pier.

Judging by the picture, Tad had been what my grandmother would have called "a good-looking devil." By that she would have meant handsome, of course, but more than that. Even in a black-and-white photo, Tad had a broad and confident grin. He looked as if he could sell cars with great success. Not so strange, since Tad had turned out to be an army sergeant. One of my Texas uncles had spent nearly thirty years as a noncommissioned officer. He had always assured the family that the NCOs ran the army, from the newest enlistee to the top general. A career like that requires confidence.

Though I had never met Tad, I had known his dad slightly. Tad looked like him, with sandy hair. Tad's list of activities included football captain, vice president of student council, and president of VICA, a club that required part-time work. How had he found time to fool around with the Sharks?

The next Shark, alphabetically, was Sharpy Brock. Sharpy had looked bookish, very serious. He had dark-rimmed glasses, and his expression was almost grim. Had his appearance guided him into his scholarly career? He had taken part in drama club, with a leading role in two plays, and he was on the golf team. He was an officer of the student council.

The third Shark, Chip Brown, looked nothing like his brother, Digger. Digger had a scrawny look, but Chip was slim. Odd, I thought, both adjectives refer to slenderness, but one was a compliment, and the other was not.

Chip had definitely been a good-looking young man. His hair was blond and neatly trimmed, and he had a winning smile.

Had his mother made him clean up for his senior picture? Or did he look neat all the time?

Digger, of course, today usually looked as if he hadn't had a shower or washed his hair for a month. Warner Pier's yearbook included middle school as well as high school, so I flipped back to the seventh grade and found him. No, I decided, there was no help for Digger; he looked scrawny and dirty at thirteen, and he still looked that way today.

Chip had played varsity basketball and founded the Spanish club. He was also president of Warner Pier High Service Club, which organized activities such as food drives or cleanup projects.

I skipped over Brad Davis, since I'd seen what he looked like in the present, and turned to Spud. Poor Spud. Nobody had liked him today, but in high school he must have had some appeal. After all, he was a Shark!

And Joc had told me Spud was very popular in high school. Now I could see that he had been a good-looking guy, despite the oval head that reminded me of a fish. Joe had also said he was known as a joker, a clown. A sense of humor was definitely an asset in making friends. And if you were in a sales career, it could also lead to customers.

But why would a Realtor sock cash away in a little safe? He should have understood the value of earning interest.

I glanced at the list of activities under Spud's picture. Interestingly enough, Spud had been editor of the yearbook and vice president of the Honor Society. He'd also been an officer for the service club. But he remained a mystery to me.

I declared Spud an enigma and turned back a page to Brad Davis.

JoAnna Carl

On the face of things, today Brad had everything. He came from one of the wealthiest and most respected families in the area. He was reasonably good-looking. He had received a top-notch education. He had a beautiful wife, and they lived in a beautiful home with their two beautiful children. He even had an elevator to his office.

I read the bio under his senior picture. "Brad may well be called a proud son of Warner Pier," it said, "since his ancestors were among our earliest settlers."

I wondered if that knowledge weighed on Brad. It was certainly a situation that could cut both ways, either inspiring service to the community your ancestors had established or causing the family heritage to weigh you down.

Brad had gone out for basketball every year and had been a founder and president of Warner Pier High Service Club—a suitable activity for someone who would later be in charge of the area's largest charitable organization. He had also been president of the Honor Society.

The lights of a car flashed into the living room. I closed the yearbook. *It must be Joe.*

I met him at the back door. "You're home!"

"I'm glad you're pleased to see me. Or are you angry that I stayed so long?"

I laughed. "Both, I guess. But mainly I've entertained myself with your old high school yearbook."

"Oh, good night! Wasn't there anything on television?"

"Not much. Are you ready for a truffle?"

"Sure. But I need to check the mail. Did I get a letter from the Chicago lawyer?"

"You only got one letter, and I don't think it had a printed return address. That doesn't sound like a lawyer."

"I'll check it." Joe picked up his lone letter. He frowned as he looked at it. "This looks more like a crank letter than a legal document."

He reached for the letter opener and ripped the envelope open. He read the letter, frowning more each second, then threw the paper down.

"Damnation!" he said.

"What is it?"

"You can read it!" Joe tossed the letter across the table.

The letter was written on notebook paper, in pencil.

Watch out, Tater. You could end up like your pal.

Chapter 18

"What is the deal with this Tater!" Joe yelled the words. "I never met a Tater in my life. What is going on?"

I was amazed—at the threat and at the use of "Tater" in the threat. But maybe the most surprising thing was Joe's anger. He's normally a calm person.

"Whatever is going on," I said, "this was a threat. We need to report it to Hal Haywood or to Hogan or to both of them."

So we did. I made the call, and I made it to Hogan. "We can't understand why the name 'Tater' is used again," I said. "Joe says he's never used the nickname and neither has anyone he's ever known. But obviously someone thinks he has."

"I'll talk to Hal," Hogan said. "We'll come by tomorrow and pick your brain. For tonight I'll put a patrol car in your neighborhood."

He made a few other soothing noises, all about how people who intend to do harm will do it, not talk about it. Et cetera. He assured us that there was very little chance that Joe and I could be in danger.

I didn't find it very reassuring.

Joe wasn't reassured either. He paced around the house, growling. He made a cup of instant coffee, then didn't drink it. He refused dessert, even a truffle. He glared, sometimes at me and sometimes at the pictures on the wall.

I stood it for about twenty minutes. Then I took a stand.

"Okay, Joe," I said. "If the mention of Tater is going to drive you nuts, I want to know why."

"Because it has nothing to do with either of us!"

"Then why does it upset you so?"

"It doesn't!"

"Then sit down and drink your coffee. Eat a chocolate! You're making me crazy."

He threw himself into his easy chair, scowling. He took a large gulp of his coffee. This was a mistake, since I had just re-heated it. I tried to sit there calmly, ignoring him as he gulped the hot coffee, then roared in pain. I did not laugh.

But I wanted to.

I stared at my own truffle. Naturally, it was one of the Ten-Huis Chocolade rejects: a perfectly fine chocolate with the wrong decoration.

"This," I told Joe, "is a chocolate with a key lime interior and a dark chocolate exterior. Unfortunately, it was trimmed with an orange dot, instead of a lime green one. It tastes fine but can't be sold. It's silly. But you and I will simply have to force ourselves to eat it. What a pity."

Joe gave a deep sigh and reached for the truffle. "I get it," he said. "You think I'm acting silly."

"Maybe. What you're telling me is that the nickname Tater bothers you a lot, but you don't want to admit it."

Joe didn't say anything for quite a while, and neither did I.

He sipped more of his coffee—slowly this time. And he finally spoke.

"I think what I hate is that I've been acting stupid. That's what I'm going to have to admit."

It was my turn to sit quietly then. And in another minute, he began to talk. "I know it's hard for you to see how popular the Sharks were. You weren't at Warner Pier High."

Joe went on to explain that membership in the Sharks was a cause for envy. The five Sharks—Tad, Sharpy, Spud, Brad, and Chip—had held a lot of the leadership positions in their class and in the school.

"Of course the girls had their own popular cliques.

"But to us guys the Sharks were the coolest. Everybody wanted to be like them. If one of them wore a plaid shirt, the next week half the school had plaid shirts. And the thought of gaining membership in that inner group would make any of us go nuts."

"But Joe," I said, "they were all seniors, and you were a junior. I thought they picked their members strictly among the seniors."

Joe looked uncomfortable. He dropped his eyes, drank another gulp of coffee, then took a deep breath.

"That was part of their mystique," he said. "They seemed to have been formed for that one year. After senior year, the group was going to split up, go to different colleges, into different jobs. It would be finished. Over.

"Meanwhile, Tony and I had a bunch of guys we ran around with. And there were other clusters of guys who hung out together. But nothing like the unity of the Sharks."

He took another deep breath. "Then our class began to elect

officers for our junior activities. And I got elected to several positions."

"I know, your mother loves to tell people you won honors for the debate team, captained the wrestling squad, and were class president. And I know Tony was right in there with you."

"That was the next year, our senior year." He frowned and sighed again. "This is the part I hate."

"What? Joe, what happened?"

"One night Tad Bailey asked me to come over and study with him. Some test was coming up. I was flattered. I borrowed my mom's car and drove over to the Bailey house." He stopped talking again.

"Oh, come on, Joe," I said. "You've got me all in suspense! What happened?"

"It's not worth the suspense! Actually Tad took me downstairs to that club room. The Sharks were there, and Spud—who seemed to be the leader of the group—told me the Sharks had decided that they had been so successful as high school leaders that they wanted it to continue. They were ready to handpick a group of junior class members who would become the 'new' Sharks. They'd be expected to carry on the tradition of high school success for the next year.

"I remember that he said something like, 'Then that group will pick five more Sharks to be leaders the next year.'"

He and I stared at each other. And suddenly I wanted to laugh. I went as far as a smile. "Joe, that would never have worked!"

"I know now. But at the time it was pretty heady stuff. I was quite seduced by the thought of becoming the anointed leader of the next senior class. Then I asked who they thought would be in the group."

"Obviously you."

"Oh yeah. They'd called me there to tell me that. I'm sure I fanned out my tail like a turkey cock. I asked who else they were thinking of asking to be Sharks."

Joe stopped talking, and I nudged him with a question. "Do you remember who they were?"

"No, I don't, Lee. All I can remember is who wasn't on the list."

"Uh-oh."

"Right. They skipped Tony. My best friend. They didn't think he was worthy of being a Shark!"

"How did you react?"

"I think I just sat there when they listed the names. Finally I asked if they had overlooked Tony.

"They sort of looked from one to the other. Bouncing their looks around, not meeting each other's eyes. And I realized that they had deliberately left Tony out. Then they began to mumble around. Tony wasn't much of a student, someone said. He didn't plan to go to college. Tony was popular, true, but . . . But. But. But.

"Finally Spud was the one who said what was on their minds."

"I think I know what's coming."

"You probably do. Spud told me that Tony was a great guy, but he was 'just a Mexican kid. Not leadership material.'"

"Did you get up and walk out?"

"That's what makes me so ashamed, Lee. I didn't. I told them I needed to think it over. I got up and left then. It was the next day before I told them I didn't want to get involved."

"That was the right thing to do."

"Yes, but I'd known that from the first moment I realized Tony wasn't in the group. And I just sat there. I've always been ashamed that I hesitated. But I called Tad the next day. Then I did tell him I thought the idea of handing down the Shark organization was a loser. And they did give it up. Or I think they did. I never had anything else to do with them until all this came up."

"What did this have to do with Tater?"

"Oh, that was even dumber. You know how every member of the Sharks had a silly nickname?"

I nodded.

"They told me that my nickname was going to be Tater."

Tater? I had married a man who could have been cursed with the nickname of Tater?

Chocolate Lore

Chocolate Affects Vision

Dark chocolate may help eyesight.

A study published in the *Journal of the American Medical Association* has shown that test subjects who ate dark chocolate before taking an eye exam did better than a group who ate milk chocolate.

Half the participants ate dark chocolate with 72 percent cacao, with total flavanols of 316.3 mg. These participants were compared with a similar group of people who ate milk chocolate with 40 mg of total flavanols.

Two hours after eating the chocolate, the vision of both groups was tested and the dark-chocolate nibblers came out on top, having better visibility of small, low-contrast targets.

Nutritionists warned that the high fat content of chocolate still leaves it a snack to be enjoyed in moderation.

Chapter 19

"Joe, they must have been pulling your leg."

"I assure you the whole thing was as serious as a heart attack. Although Spud was the most serious."

"But they could never have expected you to drop your friendship with Tony. And they definitely could not have thought you'd go along with the nickname 'Tater.'"

"They had some goofy idea about how each member of the gang was going to be some sort of a potato."

"A potato? That's stupid."

"Well, they'd already had 'Spud' and 'Chip.' Why couldn't they add 'Tater'? Then 'Frenchy,' 'Irish,' and 'Tot'?"

"Followed by 'Wedge,' 'Baked,' and 'Mashed'? Come on, Joe! It had to be some sort of joke, and you didn't fall for it!"

"I only hope you're right. That would keep me from feeling like a complete fool."

"Kids are foolish."

"Maybe so. But I'm going to have to confess to Hogan and Hal." Joe dropped his head between his hands. "I should have done that when 'Tater' first arose in that note they found with Spud's body."

"You can't do it tonight. It's nearly eleven, and I don't think either of them wants to hear about it this late."

"I guess you're right. I'll call Hogan in the morning." Joe gave a deep sigh and got to his feet. "I guess I'll go to bed."

I began to gather up the coffee cups. Poor Joe. It's awful when a youthful indiscretion comes back to haunt us. It's sure happened to me a few times. But I'm not revealing what happened or when it occurred.

I was just putting the final cup in the dishwasher when I heard Joe's phone ring. I checked my watch. Now it was after eleven. Who could be calling?

Joe had left his phone in the living room, and all I could hear from him by then was running water in the other end of the house. I went into the living room and looked at the phone. *Should I answer?*

Of course, I should. I'm too curious not to. I was already picking up the phone.

"Hello."

"Hello. I'm calling Joe Woodyard." The calm voice belonged to a woman.

"He's unavailable at the moment. May I take a message?"

"I guess I need to start with an apology. He's left several messages during the past couple of days, but I've been out of town, and I didn't get them until I returned. Joe and I were in high school together. And I've been trying to sell him my parents' house. This is Twyla McDonald."

"Oh my gosh!" I dropped the phone, then picked it up. "Hang on! I'll call him."

As I headed through the kitchen and the back hall to reach the bathroom, I clutched the phone against my chest. And I yelled. "Joe! Joe!"

I reached the bathroom door ready to pound on it, but Joe threw it open. Toothpaste was dripping over his chin.

"Is the house on fire?"

"No! It's Twyla. Twyla McDonald is on the phone."

Joe grabbed a towel and mopped his chin. I managed to punch the speaker button before he took the phone.

"Twyla! Am I glad to hear from you!"

"Oh, Joe! I hope nothing's gone wrong with the house sale!"

"Oh no. Everything's fine on that front. Have you talked to Tad?"

"No, but he's been leaving messages, too."

"Has anyone told you about Spud?"

"I had a couple of obnoxious phone calls from Spud, but that was sometime back. Nothing lately."

Joe quickly sketched the facts about Spud's death. And for once someone acted normal upon hearing about the death of an old acquaintance. Twyla greeted the news with remarks such as "oh no" and "I can't believe this."

At the end of the tale, she gave a loud groan. "This is totally amazing, Joe. It doesn't seem possible that anyone would actually get so mad at Spud that they would kill him."

"It's pretty surprising, Twyla. Of course, nobody knows why he was killed yet."

"Oh! I see what you mean. It could have been for love, for money, for some reason other than general obnoxiousness."

"True. Twyla, I need to ask you a couple of questions."

"Sure."

"The first question is, did your dad give Spud a right of first refusal letter on the house?"

"Spud said he did. He gave me a photocopy of it. Then I went through Dad's desk and found a copy. But my lawyer, in Holland, looked at Dad's copy. And he said the letter became void with Dad's death."

"Good. That clears up that possible problem. But I've got another question."

"Shoot."

"Funny you should say that. The second question is, did your parents keep a gun in their house?"

"Absolutely not! Why are you asking that?"

Joe briefly described the situation when Digger and I found the Peacemaker pistol in the basement. He did it without comment, and Twyla didn't comment in her reply.

"No, Joe. Mom and Dad didn't keep a pistol in the house."

"You're sure they didn't get one after you left home?"

"Absolutely."

Joe didn't reply, standing there silently for long enough that Twyla spoke. "Joe? Are you there?"

"Sorry. I'm just trying to figure out how that pistol got there."

"I can't solve that one. But I can assure you of one thing. That pistol wouldn't have been owned by either of my parents or by Tad."

"You're positive?"

"Yes. It's in the family lore. When my mother's brother— our uncle Frank—was ten years old, he found a pistol in our grandfather's bureau drawer. He was just a little boy, Joe. He took it out to look at it."

She took several deep breaths. "The pistol went off. Uncle

Frank was killed. Since that time no one in my grandmother's family has ever owned a pistol. It's an absolute no-no."

Joe assured Twyla that he certainly understood that reaction and that he would tell Hogan as much.

"Though Hogan will probably want to hear all these things himself," he said. "He just asked me to track everybody down."

"That's fine," Twyla said. "I'll be glad to talk to him."

They said good-bye after assuring each other that the house deal was still alive.

Joe immediately went to the bathroom sink and rinsed toothpaste out of his mouth.

I waited for him to finish, leaning on the doorframe. When he stood up, once more dried the toothpaste off his chin, and turned to look at me, I spoke.

"Interesting," I said, "that the family has this universal revulsion at ownership of a pistol."

"Understandable."

"It certainly is. But I wonder how the family reacted when Tad, Twyla's brother, put that revulsion behind him and became a professional soldier. I understand that they are required to learn to use pistols."

Joe rolled his eyes. "For tonight I don't give a darn," he said. "I've got worrying to do. Tomorrow I need to tell Hogan and Hal about one of the most embarrassing things that I ever did."

Joe didn't talk a lot more about his "Tater" complex, but he was mighty quiet before breakfast the next morning. He didn't look at all happy as he put the mysterious letter in his pocket and headed out the door.

I felt sorry about his embarrassment, but I felt certain that the friendship between Joe and Hogan would stand the strain. A little yelling, maybe. A complete split, unlikely.

So I was surprised when Joe came by my office at mid-morning and reported that the interview had gone badly.

"Ouch!" I said. "So what did Hal have to say?"

"It seems I'm a lousy piece of something disgusting, and the murder of Spud Dirk would be solved already if I had admitted I was Tater when the name first came up."

"But you weren't Tater, Joe."

"I don't think Hal believes that." A slight smile came over his face. "I think he was going to tell me to get a lawyer, but just in time he remembered that I am one."

I smiled back. "At least you haven't lost your sense of humor—completely."

"It's going fast. But once Hal had used up all his smart remarks, we had a long talk about the main problem the introduction of Tater into the situation brings up."

"I've been thinking about that, too."

"And what's your conclusion?"

"The problem is, who knew you were Tater? That person is the one who wrote the two notes. Does it have to be one of the Sharks?"

"That would appear to be the case."

"Maybe not, Joe. I've been giving the situation some thought, and there are other possibilities."

"Such as?"

"Family members, among others. If you think about how curious a kid like Digger must have been, can you believe he didn't spy on his older brother?"

Joe laughed. "No, I can't. Digger would have been eavesdropping whenever Chip was on the phone."

"Or a sister? Twyla? Or how about girls the Sharks dated? Or parents?"

"Teachers? Unlikely, but that's another possibility. And I'm sure Hogan and Hal are thinking about this."

Joe leaned forward and tapped on my desk. "But, Lee, Hal definitely thinks I'm the most likely suspect at this point. I think the only thing that stood between me and the third degree is the fact that I brought the letter in voluntarily."

"Yes, that's in your favor. But the real question is *why*? Why does the letter writer think he can scare you off simply by invoking the name 'Tater'? And why is he *so* insistent that you stay out of the whole affair?"

I leaned forward. "What does the letter writer think you know?"

Chocolate Lore

Forget What Your Mother Told You

Don't forget all of it! Most mothers know a lot—a lot more than sons and daughters give them credit for knowing.

But that old wives' tale about chocolate making your face break out is just that. Only believed by old wives. Highly unlikely.

True, some people can't eat chocolate without breaking out. Nobody can eat everything. If they think they can, it simply means they haven't yet met the food that gives them trouble.

For years I thought I had a lead stomach; impervious to digestive problems. Then avocados, which I had scarfed down for my whole life, began to lead to heartburn. Romaine got popular, and I discovered that even a small salad was a problem for me. At the risk of being thought unfashionable, I went back to iceberg.

So, be cautious. Chocolate—the food of the gods—can be linked to heartburn, migraines, and even arthritis.

And remember—chocolate can be poison to your pets.

Chapter 20

Instead of eating bonbons the rest of the morning, I chewed my nails.

If Joe were right that the state police detective was serious, that Hal thought Joe was the mysterious Tater who was involved with Spud's death, that was definitely something to worry about. Joe was in danger.

And when somebody I love is in danger, I have to do something about it. Unfortunately, in this situation I had no idea of anything that might be helpful.

Spud's death seemed to be part of a tornado of events that made no sense. Objects, ideas, and people seemed simply to fly by for no reason. Everything that had happened seemed to be nonsense.

Why had a pistol been hidden in the basement rafters in the Bailey house?

Why had Spud been so determined to buy the Bailey house, anyway?

Who had been prowling around the Bailey house the night after Spud's death?

Why had Spud hidden cash in a safe at the convenience store? Surely he could find a more secure place for his money.

Why had Spud told his wife he could force Tad and Twyla to sell their parents' house to him, even after lawyers said that the right of first refusal was no longer valid?

Who had stolen Curley McWhirley's shoes? Was it really a kid? Or a tramp?

None of it made sense.

I firmed my jaw and sat up straight. I knew Hogan was trying to find a pattern in the situation, but would he be able to do that? Joe seemed convinced that Hal was simply trying to prove him guilty. The whole thing was endangering someone I loved.

I couldn't just sit by and watch that happen. I might have promised Joe that I'd stay out of the murder in the house next door to us, but I'd never forgive myself if I didn't try to find out what was really going on.

But what could I do? I had no idea.

And at exactly that moment, an idea drove by.

The idea in question, of course, didn't look like one. It wasn't embellished with a neon sign saying, INSPIRATION! or anything.

No, it looked like a hearse. That's because it was a hearse. It was the dignified cream-colored vehicle that is usually parked in the garage of VanHorn Family Funeral Services, next to the black limousine used to carry the family to funerals and the small black sedan that Vic VanHorn, owner and manager, drove around town. A car not unlike the one our prowler had driven.

I reached for my cell phone, found a telephone number, then punched CALL. A solemn voice answered immediately. "Van-Horn Family Funeral Services."

"Hello, Vic," I said.

"Hello, Lee." Yes, about three quarters of Warner Pier recognizes my voice. Maybe it's the Texas accent?

I spoke again. "Has the time for the funeral of Richard Dirk been set?"

"Oh yes. Graveside services are to be at four o'clock this afternoon in Warner Pier Memorial Cemetery. And Lee . . ."

"Yes, Vic?"

"I hope to see you there."

"Thanks," I said, and broke the connection.

It will be interesting to see just who does show up, I thought. And whoever did appear, I intended to be among them.

As it happened, Aunt Nettie came along with me. As a lifelong resident of Warner Pier—except for that year she spent in Amsterdam learning to make chocolate—she naturally knew every soul in town. So when I told her I was planning to attend the funeral, she hopped right in the car. Well, sort of. We both did run home to change from our working clothes, which consisted of jeans and a sweater for me and a white cook's uniform for her. I substituted wool slacks for my jeans, and Aunt Nettie put on a navy blue pantsuit.

As we pulled into the cemetery, I could see a small group. I was sure it was at Spud's allotted plot; a town of twenty-five hundred was unlikely to have two funerals in one afternoon. I headed along one of the winding roads that led through the cemetery toward the dozen or so people.

"I've always wondered just why roads in cemeteries go around in circles," I said.

"I guess they're trying to look artistic," Aunt Nettie said. "I've always wondered why they have so many trees."

"Texas cemeteries don't have so many trees. At least in my part of the state. But they still have these twisty roads."

I pointed ahead. "Look! There's Hogan."

"Oh dear. He's going to want to know why I'm here!"

"And your answer is . . . ?"

Aunt Nettie giggled. "The truth. Sort of. I used to know Spud's mother. And what's your answer?"

I managed to keep a straight face. "I thought I'd pay my respects."

Neither of us was going to admit we simply were curious.

At the plot, about twenty-five chairs had been lined up in three rows. Star was standing in front of them, next to an urn on a pedestal draped in purple. Aunt Nettie and I approached quietly and went forward to greet her like perfect ladies.

"Lee?" She sounded amazed as she shook my hand. "I didn't expect to see you here."

"It just seemed to be the right thing to do," I said.

Luckily Star didn't question what I meant by that. Instead she introduced me to her mother, a tall and tough-looking gal with bleached hair and several layers of makeup. She looked like a woman who would name her daughter "Star." Star and her mother seemed to be the only family present.

As predicted, Hogan climbed out of his car and beckoned to us. We joined him, and he led us aside. "And just what are you two doing here?" he asked.

We trotted out our prepared excuses.

He frowned. "Just take a seat in the back row and stay out of my way," he said.

That was fine with me. We followed his directions, and the back-row location did prove ideal for seeing interesting things.

Brad Davis, for example. He came, and so did his father. But they arrived separately, and they barely nodded to each other. They chose seats at opposite ends of the second row.

Aunt Nettie told me the officiating minister was assistant pastor at Warner Pier's largest church. I'd seen him at community and public events, enthusiastically talking to everyone, but I hadn't known his name or profession. Other people attending seemed to represent business organizations—the chamber of commerce, the board of Realtors, the tourism committee. Even one city councilman appeared.

I wasn't too surprised to see Mrs. McWhirley, since she had told Hogan and me that Spud had grown up in her neighborhood. Like Aunt Nettie, she had known Spud's mother. She greeted me in a friendly way, and naturally she knew Aunt Nettie.

As the service began, I had a good view of the funeral director, Vic VanHorn, and my mind wandered to his place in the community. VanHorn? Did that name mean he was related to the VanHorns and the Davises, the pioneer settlers whose descendants had established the powerful VHD Foundation? But wouldn't that mean he was a relative of Brad Davis? I wondered if a family tree of the two families was available, something to explain how everyone was related.

Then I tried to pull my attention back to Spud's funeral.

It was pretty generic, but what else could I expect? I couldn't picture Spud as an enthusiastic church member. The minister probably had never met him.

At the end of the service we all stood for a final prayer, and the urn holding Spud's ashes was solemnly lowered into the small niche.

And I asked myself why on earth I had come. What had I expected to learn? Who had I expected to see there? Had I thought someone might jump up and scream "I did it!" or make some similar confession?

No, I hadn't.

I felt quite let down as we filed past Star for one final hand-shake, an ironic expression of sympathy for a former spouse. People were leaving quickly. Both Brad and his dad, I noted, were already driving away, each in his own car.

As Aunt Nettie and I walked toward my van, I murmured in her ear, "A strange collection of people. I don't know what I expected."

At that moment, a voice called my name. "Mrs. Woodyard!" I heard footsteps crunching behind me on the gravel road. "Lee!"

Turning, I saw Vic VanHorn. Aunt Nettie and I waited until he drew near.

"A very nice service," I said.

VanHorn ignored my remark. He leaned toward me and spoke quietly. "Can you get a message to your husband?"

"I can give you his business card so you can call him yourself."

"No! No! Just tell him I need to talk to him. May I come by your house after dinner? Maybe about eight o'clock? I can't get there any earlier."

"I'll check with Joe. I'm sure he'd be glad to call you."

"No. Please. I don't want any calls. If he'll just allow me ten minutes—when you told me you were coming to the service—it sure seemed like a godsend."

"In what way?"

"I need some legal advice in the worst way, and I'm sure Joe will tell me where to get it."

I'm sure I looked surprised at that remark, but I tried to sound dignified. "I'm sure Joe will be glad to talk to you, Vic. But I prefer that he approves his own appointments."

"If he can't be there tonight, I'll try tomorrow morning. I can come by. If neither of you is there, I'll understand. Just don't tell anybody about it."

He turned and walked toward Star, leaving me amazed.

I turned to Aunt Nettie, who had been listening to us. "That's one of the oddest requests I've ever had," I said.

"Shush," she said, whispering. "He didn't want you to tell anybody."

We both laughed.

Joe had the same reaction when I repeated Vic's request to him at dinner. "Why didn't he just call me? I'm in the phone book. I'm even on Facebook."

"I don't get it either, Joe. Maybe he has some sort of a complex."

"It sounds more like he's afraid his phone line is tapped. But I'm sure he has a cell phone. He obviously wants more than the name of a lawyer."

"We'll find out when he shows up."

But Vic didn't show up. Eight o'clock came and no one knocked at the door. The phone didn't even ring. Nothing happened.

At least, nothing happened until ten o'clock. Two hours later than Vic had said he would come by.

Then I heard a police radio, and lights began to reflect through the trees between our house and the road.

I looked up from my magazine. "Is that the cops?"

Joe stood up, walked out onto the front porch, and looked toward Lake Shore Drive.

When he came back into the house, he was frowning. "Something's happened down on the road," he said. "I'll get a flashlight and walk down there to see what's going on."

"I'll go with you."

"Stay here. You're in your pajamas. It's probably somebody with car trouble. Not worth getting dressed again."

Joe came back in about twenty minutes, his face grim.

"Maybe you'd better get dressed after all," he said.

"What's happened?"

"There's a wrecked car sitting at the end of our driveway."

"Oh no! Is anybody hurt?"

"One of the cops used the word 'gunshot,' and they've called an ambulance. It's a midsized black car, Lee. I couldn't get a look at the license plate."

"Oh no!"

"I'm afraid it's Vic VanHorn."

Chapter 21

One of the neighbors had been out on a late-night errand, and on the way home he stopped to check out the parked car in our quiet area.

"Actually," he had told Joe, "I thought some kids had parked there for a necking party. I'd hate to see that get started in our neighborhood. So I stopped. But when I hit the car with the light from my big flashlight—well, I could tell right away that the driver was unconscious. And when I approached the car—I've been to enough funerals around here to recognize Vic VanHorn."

A half hour later, when Hogan and Hal came to talk to us, they confirmed to Joe and me that Vic's car had been sitting beside Lake Shore Drive, headed north, or toward downtown. He was around twenty feet from our drive. We couldn't see his car lights from the house because they weren't pointed in our direction.

Vic had been in the driver's seat, with the left-hand window rolled down. He had seemed to be coming to as the ambulance arrived. Vic lived alone; his secretary didn't know that he had an appointment that evening.

Hal's first question was whether or not Joe or I had heard a gunshot. But our television had been on, our windows had been closed—neither of us had heard anything unusual.

Other cops were asking that question of other neighbors, but in October many of the houses on Lake Shore Drive were already closed for the winter. It wouldn't be at all surprising if no one heard anything.

Soon we were telling Hogan and Hal all about Vic's request to consult Joe, and the peculiar way he had made it.

Hal, oddly enough, was acting fairly friendly. This surprised me, because our story was crazy enough to make anybody doubt it.

But after a few questions from Hal and Hogan, I figured out why Hal had changed his attitude. I already knew that Aunt Nettie had heard part of Vic's request when he told me he wanted to talk with Joe. She had obviously told Hogan. So as soon as he heard that Vic had been injured, Hogan probably passed a report about Vic on to Hal.

Because of this, Hal and Hogan began their questioning from the premise that Vic had initiated the proposed contact with Joe. He had asked to see Joe. If it hadn't worked out well, it wasn't our fault.

"The whole episode is a mystery to me," Joe said. "I can't imagine why Vic didn't simply pick up the phone book or go online, find my number at either my Holland office or at the boat shop—or even here at the house. All three numbers are listed. He could have called anytime."

"And you would have recommended a lawyer? On the phone?"

"Sure. People ask lawyers for advice all the time, and they are not shy about doing it on the phone. I'd have wanted to ask some questions about why Vic wanted a lawyer. There's no use recommending a real estate specialist when the person asking needs a criminal attorney."

"Did you think Vic might need a criminal attorney?"

"The way things are going around here lately, we may all need one." Neither Hogan nor Hal reacted to Joe's remark with a smile or a laugh. Neither did I, for that matter.

"I have no idea why Vic would have wanted an attorney," Joe said. "Criminal or otherwise. There are dozens of possibilities. Vic may have had business in Chicago, for example. Sometimes people still ask me questions about Chicago attorneys, though it's been a long time since I practiced there. But Vic's problem could have been something as simple as collecting a debt from somebody in Elmhurst or Cicero. It might have had nothing to do with why he was shot."

Hal and Hogan both sighed. "Yes," Hogan said. "Not everything that happens around here involves a murder."

He turned toward me. "But I had another question for Lee."

I tried to look intelligent, but I wasn't sure I made it. I certainly wasn't feeling intelligent.

Hogan spoke anyway. "The night there was a prowler at the Bailey house—the night the guy tried to hit Joe—you said you saw some numbers of the license plate."

"I also said I wasn't sure I saw them correctly, Hogan."

He nodded. "But you thought they were three-three-one."

"Right."

"Could the letters have been *S-P-A*?"

"Spa? Like a place you get a massage? I think I would have

noticed if the letters had spelled a recognizable word. Listen, I'd love to help, but I have no idea what the letters were. Didn't y'all work out a list of plates with three-three-one? A list that covered nearly all of west Michigan? Nobody mentioned doing it, but it seems like a logical thing to do."

"Actually we did."

"Was Vic on it?"

Hogan and Hal looked at each other, apparently passing silent messages. Then Hogan spoke quietly. "Vic had access to several cars."

"I realize that. The hearse, the limo, even an ordinary car he drove. Did any of them have a three-three-one number?"

"His personal car did. The one he was in tonight."

Joe and I looked at each other. Joe shrugged.

"That Chevy? It could have been the car we saw," he said. "Of course, it could have been dozens of others as well."

"I haven't seen the car Vic was found in tonight," I said. "The one the prowler drove was totally nondescript. But why would Vic VanHorn try to break into the Bailey house?"

"That's a good question," Joe said. "There's really nothing left in it. Hogan? Can you think of anything we might have missed? Of anywhere we didn't look when we went through that house?"

Hogan shook his head. "You and I tried to clear that house out, attic to basement."

"Well, then, what could someone believe is there?"

"We didn't find anything remarkable," Hogan said. "Twyla had to hurry in clearing out the house, so she didn't get everything. We found some makeup in one of the bathroom drawers, I recall. There were some leftover paper bags in the kitchen. But nothing much, and nothing unusual. I still don't know how we missed that pistol."

"But pistol or not," Hal said, "the car and the numbers on its plate make Vic VanHorn a possibility as the prowler at the Bailey house."

Joe and I both sat quietly for at least a minute, trying to take that in. But I couldn't believe it. I simply could not picture Vic VanHorn as the prowler who was hanging around the Bailey house.

Then Joe and I both spoke at once.

"No way," I said.

"That's just not possible," Joe said.

Hal looked angry for the first time. "Why not?"

I motioned for Joe to go first.

"Vic is a tubby kind of guy. The guy I chased was thinner. True, I can't swear that he was six feet tall and weighed one-sixty. But he wasn't shaped like Vic. And he was more athletic. I'm not Superman, but I believe that if Vic swung a stick of any sort at me, I could have ducked away from it without landing on my keister."

Hal glared, and Hogan frowned. Joe gestured toward me. "Your turn," he said.

"I was the one that Vic talked to about coming out here to see Joe," I said. "We've all agreed that was a strange way to approach Joe. So why would Vic do that? Doesn't it sound more like Vic knew something about the attack, but didn't want to get mixed up in it? He wanted to tell somebody, but he didn't want anybody to know he had told."

"What could he tell?" Hal asked.

"If Vic wasn't the prowler, he might have had an idea about who was. Yes, he could have believed that there was something in the Bailey house the prowler wanted. Vic may not even have known what it was. The second possibility that leaps to mind is that Vic saw something or someone around here that made him suspicious. He might have seen somebody walking in the neighborhood. Or buying gas at the Country Store that night. Or driving a car he recognized. I'm sure both of you can think of other possibilities."

Hal frowned. "And just what would Vic VanHorn have been doing in this neighborhood himself?"

"A lot of things. He could have come to a meeting, a civic meeting of some sort in someone's home. He could have been visiting a friend. He could have gotten a call that somebody around here had died. Funeral directors probably get more middle-of-the-night calls than anybody does."

Hogan surprised me by chuckling.

"Well, Hal," he said. "I guess they're not going to buy it."

Hal gave him an angry look. "I guess not."

"Buy what?" I asked. What was up with these guys?

Then Joe laughed. "So you were trying to convince Lee and me that Vic was our prowler?"

"We thought it was worth a try," Hogan said.

"Why?" I probably sounded mad. I was. I don't like being conned. But mainly I was mystified. I kept talking. "And why does our opinion matter?"

"Because if we can convince everyone that all of us—you, Joe, Hal, and me—believe Vic was the prowler, the real culprit might come back."

Hal moved forward. "And then, young lady, we might be able to trap the guy."

Chapter 22

Of course, Joe and I said we'd cooperate. But we both had our doubts about the whole scheme.

"You might be able to sell Vic as a prowler," Joe said. "But there's no way anybody on earth would believe that he killed Spud Dirk or attacked Jerry."

And that summed it up, as far as I was concerned. When it came to violence, Vic was simply not a possibility.

But Hal and Hogan wanted to give their plan a try, so we agreed to go along with them.

Hal didn't comment on this, but merely said that he wouldn't name Vic as a suspect publicly.

They weren't asking us to do much. Mainly we were expected to act normally and live in our own house. If anybody asked if we were nervous about it, we were to say, "Oh no. The state police detectives think the illegal activities are over."

In other words, we were to lie.

And if someone asked about the murder of Spud, there was a different lie. We were to say, "Oh, the detectives have assured us that he wasn't killed there, not at the Bailey house. His death occurred somewhere else, and his body was dumped there."

Actually they had no idea where Spud had been killed. The tale was all an elaborate plan to get the prowler to come back.

"Believe me," Hal said grimly. "We're going to be waiting for him."

I didn't have the slightest confidence in Hal's scheme. But I'm no expert. It might work.

We were assured that Michigan State Police detectives were stationed in our area, but I didn't feel reassured. I don't think Joe did either. At least I heard him wake up several times during the night.

But when he came to the breakfast table, he was cheerful and assured me he'd had a good night.

"Oh yeah," I said. "That's why you were prowling around at three a.m."

"Yah, and that's why you knew I was up."

"Oh well. Life goes on. At least for some of us."

"I'm going to be working at the boat shop today. How about going out for lunch?"

"I've got to meet with Maggie and Felicia Davis. It's a Showboat committee meeting."

"You mean I'm on my own? But how did Felicia get added to the group of people working on the Showboat?"

"Apparently Brad gave her the okay to serve on Maggie's board."

"Interesting. Isn't the belief among the arts boards that VanHorns and Davises aren't allowed to take part in organizations that the foundation supports financially?"

"That wouldn't really be a practical rule, Joe. The VanHorns and Davises have been breeding like rabbits for a hundred and fifty years. Most of the population of Warner Pier must have a few bits of DNA from one family or the other. Heck, we wouldn't have any organizations at all around here unless they installed either a VanHorn or a Davis on every board in town."

"Well, there are a few of us who aren't related to them," Joe said.

"Us Johnny-come-latelies." We both laughed.

The TenHuis side of my family became full-time residents of Warner Pier after World War II. And of course, my Texas relatives had never heard of the place. Joe's family has been in Warner Pier longer than that, but not as long as the VanHorns or the Davises.

Neither Joe nor I have ever felt our non-VHD status was a handicap. We like living in Warner Pier and have plenty of friends—some of them VanHorns and Davises.

After breakfast, Joe headed for his coffee klatch of local guys, a group that includes Tony Herrera and Digger Brown, plus four or five others. He always tries to make a stop with them on the days he works in the boat shop. I tossed the dishes in the dishwasher, then went to my office.

I noticed that Joe checked all the locks on the windows and doors before he left, and I admit that I checked his check—carefully looking at both upstairs and downstairs window locks before I left for the office. The house would be stuffy when we got home, but we could live with it.

My job had received so little attention from me in the past week that I had no trouble keeping busy all morning. I was in the middle of a financial report when Bunny nudged me and told me to leave for my meeting. Then I scooted down a half block to the Sidewalk Café, where Lindy had agreed that we could hold our meeting in the restaurant's back room.

Naturally, Maggie wasn't there yet. I knew she had a class until noon, so I had expected her to be a few minutes late. But Felicia Davis was already in the little meeting room looking at the menu.

"Sorry if I'm late," I said.

Felicia greeted me with her usual friendliness. "I think you're on time to the minute. Maggie told me to order a salad plate for her. Do you need a menu?"

"We eat here so often that I have the darn thing memorized, I'm afraid. I always have vegetable soup and a grilled cheese sandwich. So, whenever you're ready, we can wave at the waitress."

"I'm ready," she said. "French dip forever."

And magically, the waitress came in and took our orders. Things always seem to be on schedule for Felicia.

Felicia is one of those people who look as if they own the world. Sleek. That's the word for her. Her hair is sleek and dark, her legs are long, her stomach flat, her face classic. But that world-owning appearance comes with more than inherited good looks. She's also calm. She never seems upset or late or worried about anything. Poise in person.

I always wonder what's going on behind that sleek, calm, poised surface. Surely, she sometimes feels hassled like the rest of us.

As the waitress left, Felicia smiled at me. "It's awful how I get in a rut, food-wise."

"This place is so close to my office that I'm here nearly every day. But it's nice to have a new face to share a table with. I know

Maggie is very pleased that you'll be joining the Showboat's board."

"I'm cautious about joining boards and committees because people tend to misunderstand. Either they think I have to get Brad's okay before I can take part in any activity, or they seem to feel that Brad's position gives me an in when it comes to backing projects."

I laughed. "You mean that neither of those things is true?"

"I'm afraid not. Actually Brad doesn't have any official say with the VHD board. His function is doing research and typing up the agenda. It's a part-time job."

"Does he have a vote?"

"No. He's just a paid employee of the foundation. Of course he can make recommendations. But to that board, he's only a kid! All of them have known him all his life."

"You mean they feel free to ignore him?"

"Perfectly free. Even obligated."

I laughed again. "There's one thing I'd like to see come to town, speaking as a relative stranger to Warner Pier."

"A good dry cleaner?"

"True! But even more than that, I could use a genealogical chart explaining how this whole town is related."

It was Felicia's turn to laugh. "As a fellow newcomer, I'll endorse that one. We've had four calls this morning to tell us how sorry people are about the attack on Vic VanHorn."

"And?"

"We're not related to him!"

I leaned forward. "You're not?"

"No. Bradley's mother was a VanHorn, but it was a different family. No relation at all."

"I see. So when it comes to the VHD Foundation, Brad's a Davis, but not a VanHorn?"

"He's neither, actually. Well, Brad's mother was a member of the so-called real VanHorn family, the one that is descended from the original pioneers. But his dad—Drew is originally from New England. He has no relationship to the Warner Pier Davises. He's a newcomer like me!"

"I guess I just assumed he was a native Davis. Dumb."

"Of course, Davis is a common name everywhere, Lee."

"It was simply stupid, however. But not the stupidest thing I've ever done."

"I don't tell the stupidest thing I ever did," Felicia said.

"Neither do I." Maggie's voice sounded behind us, and she came in the door, leaving it ajar behind her. "Now that we've told all our secrets—or haven't told them—we'd better get started. Edna called to say she was on her way."

"Edna?" She hadn't mentioned any Edna earlier. "Edna who?"

"I'm happy to tell you Edna McWhirley called this morning and agreed to serve on the board."

Chapter 23

"Edna McWhirley?" I'm sure my voice was amazed, but Maggie still sounded calm as she repeated the name.

"Dr. Edna McWhirley," Maggie said. "Professor emeritus of speech and drama at Southwest Michigan College."

Felicia's voice also remained calm. "Emeritus? When did she retire?"

"Last June," Maggie said. "As for the Showboat board, I caught her at a brief moment when she was still feeling that she might have trouble keeping busy."

"I won't tell her," Felicia said, "but keeping busy won't be a problem. Warner Pier is waiting to pounce on her."

They both laughed, and I chuckled, although I had no idea what I was laughing about. When the giggling stopped, I decided I'd better ask.

"The only McWhirley I know in Warner Pier is the widow of Curley McWhirley," I said. "Is this the same person?"

"Sure is," Felicia said. She smiled at me. "I see you've heard about the notorious Curley. I assure you that Edna is quite a different type of person."

"Oh, I've met her," I said. "And she seemed to be a sensible, levelheaded woman. As a matter of fact, she's coming in the outside door right now."

I was able to wave to Mrs. McWhirley—I mean, Dr. McWhirley—as she approached. She came into the meeting room smiling that sweet grandmotherly smile she had when Hogan and I interviewed her two days earlier.

I was astonished by the whole turn of events.

Of course I saw the value of having a retired speech and drama professor on Maggie's board. That part was easy.

The hard part was picturing that sweet person Hogan and I had met as a highly educated college professor. I would have expected her to be baking cookies and knitting baby blankets while catering to a notoriously "cranky" husband.

But I knew all types of people could have surprising personalities and interests, so I kept my mouth shut and told Dr. McWhirley it was nice to see her again.

The meeting went smoothly, as Maggie's meetings always do, and within the hour our next jobs were assigned and each of us had eaten lunch. I didn't really have a chance to talk to Dr. McWhirley until the meeting ended. She was parked, she said, in front of TenHuis Chocolade, and she'd be delighted if she could walk with me as she went to her car.

"I hadn't realized you were a college professor," I said. "What was your specialty?"

"I mainly taught introductory speech classes. Plus, I chaired the speech camp and some of the competitions. I particularly enjoyed working with non-majors. But that's not why I wanted to speak to you. I wanted to thank you."

"What for?"

"For coming along with your uncle and acting sympathetic."

"I hope I am sympathetic! Your concerns are completely understandable."

"Well, Chief Jones did show more interest than previous law officers have. I know it's stupid to be concerned about a pair of shoes. Shoes that disappeared twenty years ago!"

"It doesn't seem stupid to me. True, it's not as if shoes were some historic relic to be handed down to your descendants, but I'm like you. I like to understand just why things happen."

Dr. McWhirley smiled. "I guess that's what I liked about working with the kids at camp. The young students are like toddlers, always saying, 'Why?' Or the smart ones are. They're completely caught up in what causes things to happen."

"You mean, why do people do the things they do?"

"Right. In drama, of course, that's a key issue. But even in speech. Why does one argument convince and another fail to convince? Why does a particular example catch the listener's ear? How do you avoid clichés? Or can they be used in effective speaking?" She shook her head. "Of course, some people never really understand. Like Spud."

"Spud Dirk? Was he one of your students?"

"Not really. But Curley and I knew him, since he lived close to us. And he tried to become an effective communicator. He read tips, such as 'you' is the most important word, or it's important to have a firm handshake, and he'd try to follow that."

"I always felt that those rules didn't work unless they reflect a genuine interest in people."

"True. And I'm afraid Spud never really caught on to that. I believe that he truly liked Curley though."

"Oh?" I started to go on, but abruptly shut my mouth. I was afraid to say anything about Dr. McWhirley's husband. Everything I'd heard made him sound like a louse.

I think she understood my difficulty, because she smiled at me, her eyes twinkling. "Curley wasn't as awful as his reputation," she said. "He genuinely liked young people. He was a scoutmaster for ten years, for example. And his troop was quite successful."

I was surprised by that news. "Very interesting," I said. "Was Spud a Scout?"

"Yes, he was. Because he lived so close to us, he was one of Curley's main assistants. We rather enjoyed him—despite his insincerity. And I always thought he enjoyed Curley."

"I'm sure he did." She had made me curious. "Just how close did Spud live to you?"

"Oh, I sometimes call it 'next door,' but that's an exaggeration. Our house is nearly a quarter mile off Lake Shore Drive, and Spud's family lived a couple of hundred yards beyond us."

She sighed. "When I describe it that way, it doesn't sound close at all. But Spud had to walk down our drive and come quite close to our house when he came and went. So we saw a lot of all the Sharks, since Spud didn't have a car, and all the Sharks were good about giving him rides."

"I see. In my high school that would have been a big problem."

"It's a big problem in Warner Pier, too. Especially since Spud's mom had to work nights. So he walked a lot, unlike some kids. Both Curley and I always tried to look out for him, offer him a ride. I guess we felt that he needed a friend."

"Spud wasn't close to his parents?"

"His father was dead by that time. His mother worked two jobs, and she wasn't—well, she wasn't very communicative. Simply not a person who had much to say. I always felt his isolation was one reason he got so involved in that gang."

"I can see that."

"But Curley tried to be friendly with him. And Spud seemed to appreciate his efforts." She sighed, then spoke again. "I'll never forget how stricken Spud looked the night they found Curley's body."

"I can imagine!"

"I truly appreciated him that night. When the ambulance came, he walked down to the place where Curley was found. After they had taken Curley away, Spud offered to stay with me. But my sister had arrived, and we went to the funeral home."

That surprised me. I thought the ambulance would have taken Curley's body to the hospital. "Straight to the funeral home?"

"Yes, since Dr. Davis had stopped to see what the emergency was, he was able to certify Curley's death as a heart attack right on the spot."

Dr. McWhirley had grown sad as we talked, but now she smiled her sweet smile. "I'm sorry, I rarely let myself get maudlin over Curley's death!"

"That's quite all right. I hope I'm a good listener."

I realized that she and I had reached TenHuis Chocolade; we were standing right in front of my office.

Impulsively, I hugged her. "I'm so glad we're going to be serving on Maggie's committee together," I said. "It's going to be fun to get acquainted with you."

I stood on the sidewalk waving as she drove away. *Poor woman*, I thought. It would be hard not to get maudlin over someone who died in such an unusual way. Imagine. Dying of a heart attack while on a walk prescribed by his doctor.

A rabbit ran over my grave, and I shivered all over. Weird.

And to think that this episode occurred the same night that the Sharks staged the fake holdup at the Country Convenience Store. Weird and weirder.

And Spud, what about him? Had he witnessed both events?

That was beyond weird. It was downright hard to believe there was no connection.

I felt a sudden need to talk to Joe. Maybe he could convince me that Spud's presence at both the fake holdup and at the death of Curley McWhirley was just a coincidence.

Chapter 24

I worked diligently until closing, but on my way home I simply turned my imagination loose. I thought about all the crazy things that had happened the night of the mock holdup, including the night's final and craziest event—the discovery of Curley McWhirley lying dead beside Lake Shore Drive. Shoeless.

It seemed bizarre to me that two such weird things could happen in the same area, around the same time. Yet everyone who had been around then simply accepted that they had. Now I was wondering if those two events could be connected to the death of Spud Dirk. And beyond that, could Spud's murder be connected to the attack on Vic VanHorn?

My imagination balked. I kept picturing Frozen Rainbow pouring onto the floor of the Country Convenience Store, Curley eating a forbidden Hershey bar, the Sharks dressed in hoodies and bandannas, the mild-mannered Bradley pulling out a pistol from under the counter. How could those things be linked to Vic taking me aside at Spud's funeral and telling me he needed to talk to Joe?

Unbelievable.

One of the pictures that kept popping into my mind was Edna's memory of Spud on the night her husband died.

Most sixteen-year-olds would have been knocked in a heap by the events of that evening. No wonder Edna recalled Spud as looking shocked. He must have been walking back from the fake holdup when he stumbled upon the ambulance picking up her husband. Unless one of the Sharks gave him a ride.

Perhaps Dr. Davis had still been on the spot, having just declared Curley dead. Or was the doctor at the McWhirley house? Had he gone there to tell Edna what had happened to her husband?

Where had Brad been while this was going on? Had he been cleaning up the Country Convenience Store? In his place, I certainly would have insisted that my friends help. After shooting the Frozen Rainbow machine, surely they hadn't run off and left him with the mess of icy goo.

I wondered how the other boys had reacted when they heard Curley was dead—did it make them forget the holdup and how scared they must have been when the shooting started? Or had the shooting burned the event into their memories? Or had any of them even cared? After all, Curley wasn't a popular person around Warner Pier, and his death was natural. They might not even have heard about it for several days. Or did Spud tell them right away?

Had the personality of each of them been permanently marked by the gunfire that erupted during the prank? Or was youth so resilient that each had laughed the whole event off?

Edna still couldn't forget her husband's missing shoes. Brad kept mum. His father seemed to refuse to recall that the prank holdup ever happened.

How had Spud reacted?

I had reached that point in my musings when I pulled into my own driveway. I was glad to see that all the outside lights were on, and Joe's truck was already in the drive. Even though we had been assured that a "guard" from the state police would be on duty, I hadn't been eager to come home to an empty house, knowing that a man had been shot less than twenty-four hours earlier at the foot of our drive.

I felt even better when Joe came out onto the back porch and stood there, waiting for me to come into the house. I gathered up my belongings and got out of the car.

And at some moment between getting out of the car and reaching the kitchen door, I came up with yet another question. One I asked Joe as I stepped onto the porch.

"How can I get a look at all the police reports for the night that Curley McWhirley died?"

"And I'm glad you're home, too," he said with a wry look. "Do I get a kiss?"

I gave him a big one, right on the mouth, and a second under his right ear. Then I whispered, "I sure was happy to see all the lights on and you standing on the porch."

"Glad to be of service. But what's all this about police reports?"

"I just got to wondering," I said. "But maybe we could have a glass of wine while I describe the wild imaginings I had on the way home."

Joe popped a cork on a bottle of Michigan wine, and I sliced up some cheese. Then we sat in the living room, and I described the things that had been running through my mind.

I ended with my conclusion. "It's simply too crazy, Joe." I

said. "Unbelievable! That much nuttiness simply couldn't go on in less than a square mile in less than an hour without being linked in some way."

"At the time nobody questioned any of it, Lee. I certainly didn't."

"You were at wrestling camp in Kalamazoo, right?"

Joe nodded. "And when I got home, my mother didn't mention any of the commotion. I didn't even know that Curley Mc-Whirley had died until the *Warner Pier Gazette* was delivered on Wednesday. And Mom didn't know about the fake holdup, so she didn't tell me anything about that."

"How did you find out about it?"

"Oh, it was all the talk at the Corner." Joe grinned. "You won't have heard of that place. It disappeared about ten years ago, but at the time it was the social center for the high school crowd. Sort of like the old-fashioned ice cream parlor."

"What did you hear?"

"We had a firsthand account from Sharpy Brock and a different one from Brad."

"So their stories didn't match?"

"Not in details. But they were good-humored about it. Brad denied he'd been scared, of course. He claimed he was only doing his duty and protecting his father's property."

"His father? What property did Dr. Davis own?"

"Didn't I tell you Dr. Davis owned the Country Convenience Store? I suppose that's why Brad was working there."

"No one's mentioned it to me. And I don't think that Hogan knew it either. I wonder how Spud got hold of it."

"Does it matter?"

"Probably not. What else was said at the Corner?"

"Oh, not much. Tad claimed that Chip wet his pants. Chip claimed that Tad was the one with the bladder problem. Sharpy said that he borrowed a hoodie from Digger, so the sleeves of his sweatshirt barely covered his elbows. The stories got wilder and wilder. I never completely believed any of them."

"Did anybody say who cleaned up the Frozen Rainbow?"

Joe frowned and sipped his wine, thinking. "I don't think that came up. At least, I can't remember anything about it."

"What did Spud have to say?"

"I don't think he was at the Corner the night I heard about it.

"It was a major event in the lives of Warner Pier's teenagers, but on the other hand, as I said, the death of Curley didn't raise a lot of interest. We'd heard of him because he was a town character. But none of us cared about his fate."

"Except Spud."

"Maybe. They were neighbors."

"And it appears that Curley took a real interest in him."

"Spud's dad had died while Spud was still in elementary school. Of course, my dad had died when I was even younger, but my grandfather filled the gap. Spud didn't have anybody like that."

"So a friendly neighbor might have been important to Spud."

Joe nodded. "That's true. I remember that Curley was a scoutmaster. I think I did know that Spud was in his troop."

Joe took another sip of his wine. "How about we quit drinking and start eating?"

I didn't argue. Joe finished preparing the dinner of deli roast chicken and five-minute mac and cheese while I put my belongings away and changed clothes. Then we ate our dinner.

The only problem was—I couldn't get the idea of a link

between the fake holdup and the death of Curley McWhirley out of my mind.

How could the two events have any relationship? The question nagged at me.

Joe tried to start a conversation, but it was an uphill struggle for him. I didn't talk about the two cases again, but I couldn't get them out of my mind. No matter what Joe brought up, what interesting comment he made, all I could think about was how those two events could happen on the same evening and not be connected.

Finally Joe spoke. "Lee! Wake up!"

I woke up, found myself staring at a bowl of melted ice cream, and couldn't figure out where it had come from.

"I'm sorry, Joe," I said. "I just can't get something Edna McWhirley said out of my mind."

"What was that?"

"I told you. She said she would never forget how bereft Spud had seemed the night Curley was found dead."

"Okay," Joe said. "That's it! Get your jacket. You and I are going over to talk to Hogan. And maybe your aunt Nettie. If they can't talk sense to you, it's hopeless."

Chapter 25

Hogan and Aunt Nettie greeted us nicely and invited us in. No, he didn't have a report on Vic VanHorn, Hogan told us. This convinced me that law enforcement had Vic under cover somewhere. I didn't ask for more details.

Then Joe made me state my concerns for them. They listened patiently, the way they always do, bless 'em, and neither of them made any comments, at least at first. But my ideas began to seem pretty dumb to me.

Twenty years earlier, two dramatic events had occurred on the same evening. First, a rural convenience store had been hit by a mock holdup. Second, a heart patient had died during his supposedly therapeutic evening walk.

Now, after twenty years, Spud, the only person thought to have been present at both events, had been murdered. How could the events *not* be connected?

At least Hogan didn't laugh. "There's no apparent connection, Lee," he said. "But you're asking a very good question. I don't think that law enforcement at the time knew that Spud Dirk was present at both events."

"Wouldn't Edna have known?" Joe asked.

"Certainly not at the time," I said. "Edna wasn't at the convenience store. All she knew was that Curley went out for a walk. The next time she saw him, he was dead.

"Of course, there's a good reason for Spud to be there; he *had* to pass the site of Curley's death on his way home. That's probably all it was. Besides, didn't you tell me you looked at the police report on Curley McWhirley's death? Did it tell about Spud?"

"It lists Spud as a witness, but no statement was taken," Hogan said. "There's nothing in it that indicates a crime was committed at the store *or* at the site of Curley's death. You're certainly welcome to look at the report on Curley's death."

"What about the prank holdup at the Country Store?"

"No one reported it. I suppose it could have been reported as malicious mischief, or something like that, but there was no particular reason to do that."

"Especially with Dr. Davis involved." I probably sounded a little cynical.

Hogan narrowed his eyes. "I can't fault Dr. Davis's actions. The only damage was to property he owned, so it was his call. Wouldn't most fathers want to avoid publicizing a practical joke his son was involved in, especially since he was the butt of it?"

Joe leaned forward. "But Brad actually fired a couple of shots!"

"You're right," Hogan said. "But no one got hurt, and it was perfectly legal for Dr. Davis to let it go. There's no evidence that Curley McWhirley was present at the store, that he was injured in any way, that he had anything to do with a silly prank. No one else was injured. There was no reason to file a complaint."

"Even though a shot was fired? And a real shot, too. Not just a BB, like the other boys fired."

"Lee, at that time the store was outside the city limits. I'd like to see you forbid firing a shot on any citizen's own property in a rural area."

"True." I sighed. "So, you're saying I'm just being over-imaginative in linking two unrelated events."

Hogan sat back in his chair. He frowned. He sipped his coffee. But when he finally spoke again, his voice was firm.

"Lee, I think that you're raising a good question, one that needs to be explored. My problem is Hal."

"The Michigan State Police detective?"

"Right. He's a by-the-book guy. I tried discussing the convenience store stunt with him, and he's just not interested. There are no written records to consult because no report was filed. And because members of my family and I myself are involved in the site where the pistol was found, I had to step aside. Hal is the lead detective in this matter. I can't just go off on my own and ignore what he says."

He cleared his throat. "Actually maybe there's no *legal* reason I can't do that. But it would put a strain on the relationship between the Warner Pier PD and the state police. And we need to keep friendly."

Joe asked the next question. "So we ignore it?"

"Certainly not. You and Lee can ask all the questions you want to." Hogan grinned. "I'd like to hear what the Sharks have to say."

Joe and I finished our coffee and started for the door. Hogan made only one more comment. "Just keep a low profile. We don't want any more killings."

Joe and I said thanks for the advice and headed for home.

Neither of us had anything to say on the trip.

Neither of us was a law officer or a detective. What would we be doing investigating crimes?

I certainly wanted to know the answers to the questions I had asked Hogan. But I wanted him to figure them out. He was used to dealing with crimes, even murders. I wasn't. I didn't want to be.

Joe and I both remained silent until we were in the house. Then Joe pulled out his cell phone and compared it with the wall calendar in the kitchen, the one I try to match with my office calendar.

"What are you doing?" I asked.

"Trying to see if my calendar's clear before we start trying to call these people."

"What people?"

"The Sharks, Lee. Somebody has to question them, and Hogan made it clear it isn't going to be him."

"Are you serious?"

"Sure. Hogan told us there's no reason we can't do that."

"He also told us to be careful."

"I don't think there's much danger with Sharpy, Tad, or even Chip. None of them seem to have even been around Warner Pier when Spud was killed and Vic attacked."

I frowned. "How about Digger? He was here."

"Digger is a maybe, I suppose, but we can start with the others." He went to the dining table—which doubles as a desk—and dug through papers until he found a yellow legal pad. "What's your first question?" he asked.

"About the put-up holdup?"

"Exactly."

I looked at Joe, thought a minute, and took a deep breath. "Okay," I said. "As long as your calendar's clear. My first question is, who had the brilliant idea of kidding Brad by pulling a fake holdup?"

"Good start," Joe said. He sat down at the table and wrote the question out in his indecipherable scrawl. "What's your second question?"

"How was the plan developed?"

Joe nodded and wrote again. "How about, did anybody know about it outside the Sharks?"

"And another question: Did these events have anything to do with all the other Sharks turning on Spud?"

Joe tapped his ballpoint on his teeth. "Or maybe, just, why did the Sharks stop being friends with Spud? Did their feelings for him have anything to do with that particular evening?"

We continued framing questions for about twenty minutes. Then we made a final list of people who we felt sure knew about the plan or who might have known about it, namely, the Sharks—Sharpy Brock, Tad Bailey, Chip Brown, and Brad Davis—and Shark siblings—Digger Brown and Twyla McDonald. Plus Star Dirk. She wouldn't have been a participant, but during ten years of marriage to Spud, she could have learned a lot.

Questioning these people might turn up additional people who could know more; people such as other spouses, parents, or best friends.

We would, we decided, start with Tad Bailey. He had been fairly cooperative during our previous call. His sister, Twyla McDonald, had been helpful, too.

There was, however, one problem. By now it was ten o'clock. Nine o'clock for Tad. A bit late to be calling Sharks, especially ones who were likely to be planning to get up early.

"Tomorrow," Joe said. "Tomorrow is Saturday. We'll call Chip in the morning. Surely he can talk on a weekend."

On Saturday morning, we got up, made sure our questions were organized, and started calling around nine thirty a.m. Sure enough, when Joe punched in Chip's cell phone number and put the phone on speaker, he answered immediately.

That was the good news. The bad news came with Chip's first sentence. "Hi, Joe," he said. "I may not make much sense. I'm in the car headed to Ann Arbor. I'm taking my boy to see his first M-go-Blue game."

Football. Autumn's curse. How had I forgotten? After all, I was married to a University of Michigan grad.

If I'd had a knife handy, I might have cut my wrists. And Joe's face looked as if he could—to quote my colorful Texas grandma—cut his suspenders and go straight up.

"Oh no!" Joe said. "We've been so involved with this mess over Spud that I haven't even read the paper or caught the sports news all week."

"But you're an alum, Joe! And they're playing Kentucky!"

Joe laughed, though he didn't sound very amused. "I can't believe I forgot. What time do you think you'll be home?"

"Pretty late. We have to stop at my wife's folks' on the way. What do you need?"

"More questions about Spud. How about if I call you in the morning?"

"Not too early!"

Joe and Chip exchanged "M Go Blue" cheers and hung up. Joe and I burst into laughter.

When I could talk, I said, "Not off to a good start."

Joe shook his head. "I should have thought about that. Let's try Tad. Maybe they don't have football in Oklahoma."

"Are you kidding? This could be OU-Texas weekend."

Lore

Sharks in Lake Michigan?

One of the most popular slogans for Michigan tourism is "Lake Michigan—Unsalted and Shark Free."

Most people laugh when they see it. Sharks lurk in saltwater oceans and seas, right? Lake Michigan and the other Great Lakes are freshwater. So no one's ever reported seeing a shark in one of the Great Lakes, right?

Well, not more than a few thousand people. These shark reports are called "urban legends."

My favorite is the tale of a boy who in 1955 was reportedly attacked by a shark. In some versions, he lost a leg. In others, he was not seriously injured. In no version did any scientist or reputable journalist ever interview him.

Some shark fans point to bull sharks, supposedly seen near Saint Louis after swimming six hundred miles up the Mississippi River. Or perhaps a shark swam a thousand miles through the Saint Lawrence Seaway—conquering locks, rivers, all five Great Lakes, and Niagara Falls—to get to Lake Michigan. But the water there is too cold for their species to survive.

So here's a salute to the five Sharks in *The Chocolate Shark Shenanigans*: Tad, Chip, Buzz, Spud, and Sharpy. Long may they live, in fiction, as Lake Michigan's only sharks.

Chapter 26

We were still laughing over our football schedule error—wondering how a Michigander and a Texan could forget the main point of fall Saturdays in the United States—when the phone rang.

Joe punched the accept button. "This is Joe Woodyard."

"This is Jim Brock. Are you the Joe Woodyard I went to high school with? And did you call me about a million times?"

"Sharpy! Wow! I'd given up finding you. And I think I called only a couple of dozen times. Where are you?"

"Home. Rolla, Missouri. But I have been out of pocket. I had a bunch of students out on a field trip. I teach geology, you know."

"No, I didn't know. The last time I heard of you, you were at Michigan State, major undisclosed."

"I'm still at an *M* college. Missouri Science and Technology. I'm sorry I didn't answer earlier. Our field trip took us so far back in the Ozarks the cell phone service wasn't any good. I didn't try to check the landline until I got home. And my wife was out of town, too. Where are you?"

He and Joe talked about five more minutes, covering the past twenty years of their lives, before Sharpy asked Joe why the heck he had called. The answer got complicated, of course.

Joe rapidly related the events of the past week, skimming over the death of Spud, the complicated happenings that followed, the attack on Vic, and the reason he was calling (Joe's friendly relationship to the Warner Pier Police chief). He left out the part when Digger dropped the Colt and it nearly shot me.

Sharpy said it was all news to him. "Since my folks retired to the Gulf Coast," he said, "I don't hear anything about the old hometown."

Finally Joe got down to business. "Sharpy, do you remember the crazy night when the Sharks pretended to hold up Brad Davis?"

Sharpy chuckled. "Oh yes. And Brad shot the frozen drink machine. I'll never forget that one. It's a miracle that no one was hurt."

"Do you remember how the plan to hold up Brad—"

"To *pretend* to hold him up."

"Right. To pretend to hold him up. How did all that come about?"

"Why do you want to know?"

Then Joe patiently took the time to explain. Sharpy didn't sound convinced. But finally he agreed to discuss it. Joe turned on the recorder and picked up a ballpoint, ready to take notes.

The idea, Sharpy said, had been Spud's. It was inspired, as Joe had recalled, by Brad's fear of being held up. "Buzz was often the butt of our jokes," Sharpy said. "He was the rich guy, of course. And he was just a little scared of getting in trouble. The rest of us weren't afraid to be reckless, as long as we didn't have to go to jail. But Buzz's dad was one of those parents who harped on 'your reputation' and 'the family's place in the community.' You know the kind."

"Sure. So what was the plan?

Chip and Sharpy each owned an air pistol, Sharpy said. Tad bought two toy guns that looked real for himself and Spud to carry.

"I think that today they'd be painted a bright color," Sharpy said. "But a toy gun that looked extremely realistic was perfectly legal in those days."

Tad was to ride with Chip. Sharpy owned a secondhand car, and he agreed to pick up Spud.

"I usually gave him a ride, because we lived fairly close," Sharpy said. "His mom had an old clunker, but she worked nights and needed it to get home."

Each Shark got hold of a dark hoodie, and each bought a red bandanna at the dollar store. Since they didn't actually plan to rob the Country Convenience Store, they didn't worry about fingerprints or other clues.

On the night when the trick was to come off, the Sharks gathered in the basement club room at Tad's house around eight o'clock.

"We checked our equipment as if we were going on a military operation," Sharpy said. "Everybody had their stuff. Then Tad told his folks we were going out for a Coke, and we headed for the Country Store.

"Joe, I want to emphasize one thing. We did not mean

to actually take anything or to hurt anybody or to do any damage."

"I'm sure of that," Joe said. "I knew you guys. You were the most law-abiding gang of delinquents I ever heard of."

Sharpy chuckled. "Maybe we were the most chickenhearted. Anyway, we parked down the road from the store, in the driveway of a cottage that had already been closed for the season. We sorta, well, tiptoed down to the store. There were a couple of cars in the parking lot—besides Buzz's—so we hid around at the side of the building. We put our bandannas on—just like Wild West outlaws—and we covered our heads with the hoodies. We must have looked like idiots.

"We huddled there until the cars in the lot had gone. Then we each took a deep breath, and we ran in the front door. And we yelled, 'Hands up! This is a holdup!'"

Sharpy stopped to laugh. "It was hilarious, Joe! I thought Buzz was going to either faint or wet his pants. His face turned green! His eyes crossed. So help me, if you've ever seen *The Wizard of Oz*—he looked just like the Cowardly Lion!"

Joe laughed, too. "Poor guy!"

"Oh yeah! I feel sorry for him now. But, you know how kids are. We were pretty merciless at the time. Then—well, that's when Buzz pulled out his pistol from under the counter and shot the poor ol' Frozen Rainbow."

"None of you knew he had a gun?"

"We hadn't had the faintest idea. I assure you we would have called the whole thing off if we'd known. It's a miracle that no one was hurt!"

"How'd you keep Brad from taking a few more potshots at you?"

"We hollered and screamed! I know I yanked that bandanna off so fast I nearly lost my nose. Everybody did. Thank God Buzz realized who we were before he took aim for a third time."

"He fired twice?"

"The first one was a misfire. Buzz told us later that the gun was his dad's. A Colt Peacemaker. Dr. Davis had told Brad that the old-time lawmen kept the chamber under the hammer empty because that model of gun was notorious for going off accidentally. So, the first time he pulled the trigger, nothing happened."

Joe looked at me and rolled his eyes. "I'll tell my wife that," he said.

Sharpy went on talking. "Dr. Davis was something of a gun collector, and Brad had snitched the gun from his dad's gun safe."

"Wasn't the gun safe locked?"

"Sure, but what sixteen-year-old wouldn't have known where to find the key? Especially in his own home? Actually I'm sure Dr. Davis locked the guns up to keep burglars from taking them. Brad was so obedient that his dad wouldn't have expected him to take one."

"I imagine you're right."

"I'm sure I am. But Brad had shown all of the guns to the Sharks a long time earlier, and we all knew where to find the key to the safe." Sharpy chuckled. "I assure you Dr. Davis didn't know that at the time, and I'm pretty sure he doesn't know it today."

"Where was the gun safe?"

"In the den. And the key was in a desk drawer. Anybody could have found them with about five minutes of effort.

Anyway, after the shooting at the Country Store, we all started to help Brad clean up. And luckily there wasn't much of a mess. When you say, 'He shot the Frozen Rainbow machine,' it sounds as if the whole store would have been covered with Technicolor goo. But in real life, the shot simply made a small hole in a small tank, and only about a quart leaked out."

Learning that made me feel deeply disappointed. I'd been picturing that "Technicolor goo."

"After we got some of the Frozen Rainbow up, Brad said that he only had two mops, and it would be better if we all left. He gave each of us a soft drink, and we went away."

"What time was that?"

"About nine. Maybe a little after. Brad said he'd meet us at the Corner after he got off work."

"Did you tell anybody about the stunt ahead of time?"

"I didn't. We were all sworn to secrecy. I felt sure that none of the other Sharks would ever speak to me again if I told."

"Did any customers come in? Either during the mock holdup or during the cleanup?"

"Luckily, no. Unless . . ." Sharpy paused, and we could hear him taking a deep breath.

Joe prompted him. "Unless what?"

"After we pulled off our disguises and everything, I thought I heard somebody in the men's room. I was worried there were witnesses to our stupid prank! But when I knocked, nobody answered, and the door was locked. I even asked Brad about it, and he got the key and checked."

We could hear another deep breath from Sharpy. "Brad didn't find anybody in the restroom. Honestly, Joe, it's hard to believe how stupid we all are when we're that age."

"That's true, Sharpy. And I've got one last question before I let you go."

"Fire away. Figuratively."

"Why did the Sharks get down on Spud? Not one of you has a good word to say about him."

Sharpy didn't answer for a long moment. "It's hard to say. We simply all began to see the jerk-ish side of his personality, I guess. He said some things about other people—well, personally, I began to think he was a liar. Anyway, you're right. We all got tired of Spud, and it broke up the gang."

Chapter 27

After Joe put the phone down, we looked at each other, and both of us shook our heads.

"Now a mysterious man in the restroom," Joe said. "What next?"

"It's hard to believe," I said. "But there's a certain logic to it."

"Why?"

"Well . . . If I was close to the ladies' room of a lonely country store, and I heard somebody yell, 'Hands up! This is a holdup!' believe me, I would be inside that door before my grandma could say, 'Lock the door.' I'd lock every bolt, and I'd yank the commode out of the floor and pile it against the door. The poor store clerk would be on his own."

"Wouldn't you call the cops?"

"Of course. If I had my cell phone. But I've been known to leave my cell phone on the dining room table when I run out to the store."

"True. And I admit I sometimes just leave mine in the car while I go inside."

"It will be interesting to see if anybody else thought there might be someone lurking in the restroom."

Joe looked at his watch. "That call took a lot longer than I expected. Is there any more coffee?"

I made another pot of coffee, and Joe looked his notes over, making sure he could read them. Then he reached for the cell phone.

"Who are you going to call next?" I asked. "Brad?"

"No, I think we should leave him until the end."

"Why? He's more likely to know about the guy in the men's room than anybody else."

"And he could say he doesn't know anything about a man in the men's room. I want all the backup info I can get before I call Brad. I think I'll try Tad."

"It's a bit earlier in Oklahoma than it is here."

"But reveille gets soldiers up at the crack of dawn."

"Not when it's Saturday and they don't live on post."

Whether reveille worked or not, something had Tad up, because he answered on the first ring. "Hi, Joe."

"I'm glad not everybody in the world has caller ID," Joe said. "Sometimes I like to surprise people. What are you up to?"

"About five-eleven, just where I was when I got out of high school. And just how many questions do you have now?"

"I'm still working on the theory that something that Spud did a long time ago caused someone to hit him in the head last week. Any ideas?"

"None at all. I told you all I know about Spud last time."

"Which wasn't much. Nobody seems to know anything or want to know anything about Spud. Why are all the Sharks so down on him?"

"We found out what a jerk he could be. It's hard to explain."

Joe paused. "This time I have a semiofficial reason for calling." He again explained that my uncle—"Chief of Police Hogan Jones"—had asked the two of us to look into any links Spud might have had with Curley McWhirley.

"We're beginning by asking everyone who was at the Country Convenience Store the night of the fake holdup to describe exactly what happened."

"Why?"

"Because that was the night McWhirley died. There's a remote chance there was a connection. Can you help us with that, Tad?"

There was a long pause before Tad finally answered. "I'll try," he said. "But I barely knew who McWhirley was."

Again, Joe started with a question about who thought up the holdup.

Again, the answer was Spud.

"Thinking back," Tad said. "Maybe— Oh, I'm imagining things, I guess. It was just that Brad was so fearful of being held up—and he was trying to hide that fear in a way that made his discomfort obvious. Does that make any sense?"

Joe said it did, and Tad went on. He explained how they all went to the dollar store for bandannas, and how they got hold of fake guns that looked real. He covered who drove—"Chip was with me, and Spud rode with Sharpy"—and he described the Sharks hiding behind the store until all the customers left.

Joe quizzed him on that point. "Both Tad and Sharpy drove? Why did you want two cars?"

"I don't really remember," Tad said. "We parked about a block down the road, at the Larkins' house. I knew that they had closed their house a couple of weeks earlier. It was still summer, but Mr. Larkin had to have surgery, so they went back to Chicago and my mom heard they weren't coming back until the next summer.

"Then all of us walked down to the store—sort of hiding. We jumped behind any handy bush if a car came along. When we got to the store, we stood off across the parking lot and looked through the plate glass windows to be sure Buzz was the only person in the store."

Then they ran in, shouting, "This is a holdup!"

And like Sharpy, Tad laughed at the memory. "Joe, I admit that was the meanest thing I've ever done. We scared Brad so bad he nearly fainted. But so help me, the look on his face was worth it.

"A moment later the shoe was on the other foot. Brad grabbed that pistol, and we all thought he was going to mow us down!"

"Sounds as if Brad had the last laugh."

"I guess you're right. I'm sure we all looked as scared as he had. I remember that Chip hit the floor behind the cigarette display."

Tad continued the story, which pretty much matched Sharpy's. The Frozen Rainbow machine was shot, he confirmed, but it had not made much of a mess. "Maybe enough to fill a big drink cup."

And the Sharks had all volunteered to help Brad clean up. "He declined," Tad said. "He said there wasn't much of a mess, and he didn't have a lot of cleaning tools. But he might have just wanted us to leave; he was pretty ticked off at us."

"Do you remember what became of the pistol?"

"I suppose Brad put it back under the counter. I don't remember anything else happening to it." Tad paused. "Actually I have a vague memory about Brad asking if anybody knew what became of it a couple of days later. But then he said to forget the question because it had turned up."

"Is there any chance that one of the Sharks blabbed ahead of time? That someone outside the gang knew about the plan?"

"I'm sure that didn't happen. Of course, we told the whole county after it was over!"

Then Joe came to the important question. "Are you sure no one else was in the store?"

"We were careful to make sure no one was there before we started the action."

"I know. But it seems funny that nobody walked in while the fake robbery was happening. You must have been there at least twenty minutes or so."

"You're right, I guess. But it didn't seem so long. And there were never many customers at the Country Store that late. That was one of the things Brad used to complain about. He said he felt as if he was wasting his time keeping the place open until ten o'clock. He said the store was deserted after nine."

"So you didn't see anybody. How about in the back room? Or the restroom?"

"No. We wouldn't have missed that!"

After that Tad promised to call if he thought of anything else, and he and Joe said good-bye.

I got each of us another cup of coffee and a piece of chocolate, and we sat and looked at each other.

"Tad was pretty sure," I said.

"Sure that there was no guy in the restroom, you mean?"

"Right. And Sharpy wasn't sure there had been. 'I thought,' he said. That's pretty vague, Joe. Do you want to call him back?"

He laughed. "No. At least not today. I'll try to call Brad."

"I've got a question," I said. "You asked it, but no one is willing to answer."

"I think I know what you mean."

"I'm sure you do. It's why all the Sharks got mad at Spud. What did he do that turned them against a brother gang member?"

Chapter 28

When Joe tried Brad's number, football again did us in. Felicia answered the phone and told us he and some old college pals had chartered a plane and flown to New Haven for the Yale-Dartmouth game.

"There are six of them. They're flying out of South Bend, and they'll head back there as soon as the game is over," she said. "Brad is planning to drive on home tonight. I'll tell him you called."

"Thanks, Felicia," Joe said. "It is rather important."

"I'll tell him that, too. And you tell Lee I'll see her at the Showboat meeting this afternoon."

She hung up, leaving me hanging in midair. I had forgotten Maggie had called another meeting on the Showboat project. When was that to be? Why were we meeting? And where?

Luckily I remembered the answers. We were once again meeting in the private room at the Sidewalk Café at noon. I was supposed to have a rough draft of our funding application ready for Maggie, Felicia, and Edna to review. With a sigh of relief, I realized I had made a start on the draft earlier. Maggie was writing up the purpose to be added to the form, but the other items were almost ready for their review.

"Well, Joe," I said, "I guess you're on your own with Hogan's project. And with lunch. I've got to go to a meeting."

He looked at me absentmindedly. "Okay. I'll see you later."

I quickly finished my draft of the grant application. Then I got dressed and headed for the meeting. I swear Joe hardly noticed me going out the door. I just hoped that whatever idea had grabbed his brain had something to do with the murder of Spud and the attack on Vic VanHorn. I was out of ideas about both.

As I started the van, I wondered why my life couldn't seem to focus on one topic at a time. The questions Joe and I were asking were important. But I couldn't think about them exclusively. No, in addition I had to think about the TenHuis Chocolade Christmas campaign, about the Showboat, and about flipping the Bailey house. Or was that the flippin' Bailey house? Sometimes my head seemed to be spinning.

Warner Pier's business district was a bit short on parking that day, thanks to the tourists who come down on autumn weekends to cruise the antique shops, admire the fall foliage, buy pumpkins, and, we hoped, stock up on chocolates. But thanks to my reserved parking place in the alley, I got situated in time to meet the others for lunch. I even had time to pick up a few goodies at TenHuis Chocolade to pass around to the rest of the committee. Plus, I actually read the menu at the Sidewalk Café. This time I adventurously ordered a French dip sandwich.

The meeting went smoothly, as Maggie's events nearly always do, and by one twenty we had approved the final VHD application. I promised to type it up neatly, and we got up to leave.

As we gathered our papers, Felicia spoke. "Lee, is an unknown killer still roaming your neighborhood? Are you scared spitless?"

I paused. That was a tricky question to answer, of course. We'd been assured that there was a guard of some sort in our neighborhood, but I couldn't tell anybody that. So I gave a vague answer.

"We've been assured that our neighborhood isn't any more dangerous than usual," I said. "Of course, this time of year we keep our eyes open for strange cars and—well, strangers of all sorts. But all we usually see are deer hunters."

"Your police chief uncle hasn't called for an armed guard or anything?"

"Good heavens, no! Naturally, since it's hunting season of some kind nearly all fall, there are already men, and women for that matter, roaming around with rifles and live ammunition. Add a few cops, and we could almost guarantee some sort of shooting incident."

"Our property is posted," Edna said. "But you know how much good that does in deer season."

We all nodded solemnly. Maggie was the only one of us who didn't live in a rural area, where deer are common. And where deer prowl, so do hunters. In season, and sometimes out of it.

I headed out of the restaurant, and Felicia, still poised, came along. "Lee," she said, "how did you get acquainted with my father-in-law?"

"Dr. Davis? He came into the shop to thank me for finding that pistol, the one that went off and nearly shot me. It seems it belonged to him."

"You didn't know him before that?"

"No, I didn't. That seems weird, since I've lived here five years, and everybody in Warner Pier knows everybody else in Warner Pier, but I don't think we'd ever met."

Felicia frowned, took a breath as if she were going to speak, then closed her mouth. We walked along silently.

I looked at her equally silently. Finally I spoke. "Spit it out, Felicia. What are you leading up to?"

"It's just silly."

"What is?"

"We had dinner at Drew's house last night, and he spent most of the meal quizzing me about you."

"That's odd. I only met him that one time, and it was, well, a very ordinary meeting. A sort of a courtesy call."

"He asked a lot of questions last night. Where were you from, how long had you lived in Warner Pier, who had you married?"

I laughed. "Did I do something that inadvertently made me appear to be smitten with his charms?"

Felicia laughed, too. "I really can't imagine that you did, Lee. To be honest, people who ask me about him usually think he's been awkward, not charming. We love him, of course, and he was a great father to Brad, especially after his mother died. Maybe a little too protective. And maybe I misunderstood the whole conversation last night."

We reached TenHuis Chocolade then, and we said good-bye. I was still puzzled as I drove home. Yes, Felicia was right; her father-in-law was often described as lacking in the doctor's traditional bedside manner. Although he lived in Warner Pier, his office and hospital affiliation were twenty-five miles away in Holland, so he wasn't a real small-town doc. Plus, Felicia had earlier mentioned he didn't grow up in our town and wasn't a member of the "real" Davis clan. It had been Brad's mom who descended from early VanHorn settlers and made her son a part of the ruling family.

I thought I had treated Dr. Davis in an ordinary way. No flirting or sneering.

I was still wondering about that at eleven o'clock that night, when Joe and I heard noises in the bushes—the bushes between our house and the Bailey house.

We were both in our bedroom, turning down the spread, when we heard rustling.

"Turn the lights out," Joe said. He jumped for the bedside lamp, and I ran for the overhead switch. With the whole house dark, we both went into the living room, where the windows faced the Bailey house.

The light on our garage didn't help. It was too far away from the lane in front of our house and from the Bailey house itself to add any illumination. On that side of the house, our windows looked out into complete darkness.

I whispered, "Did you lock up?"

"Every window, every door," Joe said. "Shush. I'm going to open this window a little. Maybe we can hear something."

He opened one of our antique casement windows a crack, and I knelt in an easy chair, leaning over the back with my ear to the window. I could hear bushes crackling and twigs breaking and gravel crunching. But there were no voices.

Then I heard a siren, not close. It gradually approached our house, and it stopped at the foot of the drive, near where Vic VanHorn's car had been found.

More crunching of gravel followed, along with some low talking.

"I'm getting my robe," I whispered. "They don't sound as if they're going to stop running around and talking anytime soon. Would we be helpful if we turned on the porch light?"

"The garage light is already on," Joe said. "I hope the noise is the cops. If they want more light, one of them will come up on the porch and ask. Or they'll call us. I'm sure they all have cell phones and flashlights."

Neither of those things happened. Instead, a spotlight of some sort swept through our trees and bushes as a patrol car came down our lane and went to the Bailey house. After about twenty minutes the voices got louder. Finally someone stepped onto our wooden porch, approached the door, and rang the bell.

Joe turned the porch light on. With the chain still on, he opened the door a crack, and we saw a state policeman outside.

"What was all the commotion?" Joe asked.

"False alarm," the cop said. "Big stag took off running. We just wanted to reassure you. There will be two patrol cars outside until morning."

Joe closed the door and turned to lean his back against it. "He might want to reassure us," he said, "but I didn't find that remark very reassuring."

"I certainly didn't either," I said. "Should we leave? I think we have enough room on the Visa to go to a motel."

"I doubt that's necessary. As long as we don't mind sleeping with the windows shut."

"And to think I moved to Michigan for the air quality."

Joe laughed. "Sure. Dead fish and sand flies. Let's go to bed."

I climbed under the covers—luckily it was cool enough that we didn't need the windows open—and I read for a long time. Now and then I heard a car pass. The sound was reassuring, and I did get some sleep. After a while.

In fact, I was still in bed when Chip called.

Chapter 29

I picked up the bedside phone and heard Joe's voice. "Hey, Chip! Go Blue!"

"A great first game for the boy kid," Chip said. "Did you watch?"

I knew that at least five minutes of football would follow that remark, so I took my time going to the kitchen, pouring myself a cup of coffee, and heading to the dining room, where I knew Joe would be ready to quiz Chip.

As I had expected, Joe had the phone on speaker, and I could hear the two guys talking about the fourth-quarter kick that saved the game for "our" side. I had barely taken a seat at the table when Joe changed the subject.

"Thanks for calling, Chip," Joe said. "Did I explain that Hogan Jones—the police chief over here—asked Lee and me to get some details on that long-ago fake holdup?"

Chip groaned. "That stupid stunt is going to haunt me the rest of my life."

"Maybe not."

Or maybe so, I thought. But I kept my mouth shut. Chip

had been warned that I was on the phone, but he was a lot more likely to talk if his old pal Joe asked the questions.

The answers were more important than the questions, of course, and Joe asked for a lot of those.

Chip's answers were pretty much the same as the ones Sharpy and Tad had offered. Yes, Spud had suggested the prank. Everybody had gotten hold of a hoodie, a bandanna, and a pistol. They had hidden the cars in the Larkins' drive. No outsider had come into the Country Convenience Store while the whole thing was going on. No, Chip hadn't suspected that there was anyone in the restroom.

Yadda, yadda, yadda.

Then Joe asked another question. "How about Digger? Did you tell him about the prank ahead of time?"

There was a pause before Chip answered. "No, I didn't tell him."

"Was there any way he could have known?"

"Sure. We lived in the same house—in fact, we shared a bedroom. All he had to do was pick up the telephone extension at the right time, and he could have known something was in the wind. But I don't think he knew any details in advance. Not from me."

"How about afterward?"

"Afterward, we told everybody. Bragged all over town."

"Yeah, I heard it myself at the Corner. But one detail seemed to be missing. The pistol. What became of it?"

"What do you mean? I assume Brad just stuck it back under the counter. Or else he took it home and put it back in his dad's gun safe."

"Actually it didn't turn up again until last week."

Joe let the silence grow. We could almost hear Chip thinking, wondering about that pistol.

Finally he spoke. "You don't mean—that wasn't the gun that went off when Digger and your wife were in the cellar?"

"I can't say that. We don't have an example of a bullet from the gun Brad fired during the fake holdup."

"But—nobody ever said anything about that gun, the gun he used that night—nobody ever said it was missing."

"Apparently it was, Chip."

"Who says? Who claims it was missing?"

"Dr. Davis. He identified it as his gun. It was reported to the national registry as a missing weapon. Possibly stolen. Dr. Davis isn't sure who reported it."

"Where was it for all these years? And why would anyone keep it? It would be easy to toss it into Lake Michigan. Bye-bye, pistol."

Joe didn't answer his questions, and Chip took several deep breaths before he spoke again.

"Are you thinking Digger might have taken it? But that's impossible! For one thing, he can't keep a secret! And why would he hang on to it, anyway? It's not as if it were used for a crime. It wouldn't be evidence of anything."

"I don't know. But I have one more question that could really be important."

"What's that?"

"Why did all the Sharks get so down on Spud? Even now, twenty years after all this happened, not one of you will say anything good about him."

"Maybe it didn't have anything to do with all this, Joe."

"It still had to do with something, Chip. What was it?"

Another long silence followed. Then Chip spoke.

"You know, Joe—I don't think we got down on Spud. Looking back, I think he got down on us. He just quit showing up. I'll think about it, and maybe I'll figure it out. But right now—I guess I've got to go."

The line went dead.

Joe's face also went dead.

I began to bluster senselessly. "What? He hung up? What in the world is going on? Is Chip crazy?" Nothing I said made sense, really. But I kept rattling on.

Joe ignored me. The more I chattered, the more he was silent. He still wasn't saying anything as he leaned over and gave me a huge kiss, right on the mouth.

That made me quit talking, of course. When the kiss ended, we sat there at the dining table, nose to nose.

"What brought that on?" I asked.

"You just looked kissable," Joe said. "I'm glad I have you."

"Or maybe you were wishing you could shut me up."

"In that case, I'd just say 'please.'" He gave me another kiss. "How about some breakfast?"

"Sure. But one question first. Do you think Digger took the pistol?"

"I'm beginning to think it's a strong possibility."

"But when did he take it? And from where?"

"I have no idea."

I considered the possibilities for a moment. "Joe," I said somberly, "do you think Digger is the killer?"

"I don't see him in that role."

"Do you want to talk to him before Brad? Or to Brad before him?"

"Maybe Brad first."

"I've got some refrigerator biscuits."

"Bring 'em on. I'll call Brad."

Naturally that didn't work out. No one answered the phone at Brad and Felicia's house.

So Joe called Digger. He answered promptly, and to my surprise, Joe invited him to breakfast.

Digger gave a deep sigh when he heard the invitation, and I began to rack my brain about a menu. A guest, even Digger, would require more food than a roll of refrigerator biscuits and a jar of preserves. Did we have any bacon? Any eggs?

Why had Joe extended an invitation to a meal? Why an invitation at all? We'd questioned everyone else on the phone.

But when Digger replied, I began to understand. "I guess it is about time we talked things out," he said.

Chapter 30

They agreed on breakfast in forty-five minutes and hung up.

"What the heck is going on?" I asked.

"I've been thinking that Digger could clear up a few mysteries and I'm not letting him leave here until I get answers."

"But you've talked to everyone else on the phone. Is there a specific reason you want to quiz Digger eyeball to eyeball?"

"I want him to trust us, not see us as the enemy," Joe answered.

"Huh?"

"We're breaking bread together," Joe said. "That's what friends do."

I couldn't argue with that. My husband had certainly taken to being a gumshoe.

"Hotcakes," I said decisively. "Everybody likes hotcakes."

That settled the menu and settled my discussion with Joe. I didn't have time to ask any more questions. I had to get dressed—no time for a shower—make another pot of coffee, cook bacon, and dig out my grandmother's recipe for Texas hotcakes. Joe set the table, opened the downstairs windows, and made a quick trip to the store for orange juice. Digger's truck was in our driveway before I had a chance to ask anything at all.

I called out a welcome to Digger. And being from Texas, I started by mentioning the weather.

"Hi, guy! Come on in! Gorgeous day. We've got the whole house open."

Digger waved at us. "Gorgeous is right. Not many October mornings when we can enjoy the sun like this in west Michigan."

I think Digger had managed a shower. He looked cleaner than I'd ever seen him. Even his fingernails sparkled, and he was wearing pressed jeans and a cheerful plaid shirt rather than his usual overalls.

Joe kept the conversation general. When Digger offered a comment about the local murder, Joe cut him off. "Hey, let's forget crime until we're through with our hotcakes."

The remark seemed to reassure Digger. Joe didn't even mention that he had talked to Chip earlier. They discussed the Chicago Cubs, cussed the government, and argued about which Michigan farm produced the best maple syrup.

They left me out of the conversation, and that suited me fine. I didn't understand what Joe was up to. I had stacked the plates in the sink and refilled all the coffee cups when he came to the point.

"Well, Digger, do you need anything more before we get down to serious conversation?"

"I've had seconds, Joe. I don't need thirds. And I do need to talk to you."

"What about?"

"That gun, of course. I feel pretty sure you've figured out how it got in the rafters."

His remark surprised me, and so did Joe's reply. "You put it there."

Huh? The pistol that nearly shot me? *Digger* had put it in the basement of the Bailey house?

Digger didn't answer Joe directly. Instead, he looked at me with a pitifully hangdog expression.

"Listen, Lee," he said, "I had no idea there was a bullet in that gun. I swear I checked all the chambers. I nearly fainted when it went off. I'm still waking up with nightmares every night."

The room should have whirled, I guess.

Was Digger telling me that he had hidden the revolver in the rafters of the Bailey house's basement? Was he saying that?

Joe told me later that I hardly reacted to Digger's apology. I know I didn't drop my coffee cup, knock over the syrup pitcher, or fall out of my chair and wind up lying on the dining room floor. But if I didn't show outward turmoil, it was because my insides had begun to churn like an ice cream freezer.

First, I told myself that I was misunderstanding what Digger had said.

Second, I felt truly stupid. Why hadn't I realized the logical explanation of how the pistol got into the rafters was that Digger had put it there?

As soon as I got to the Bailey house, Digger had told me he had known where the basement key was kept. He said he had waited outside for me, but there was no reason that couldn't have been a fib. He had had every chance he needed to hide the pistol before I got there. No wonder Joe had mentioned that he couldn't understand why—if the pistol had been there all along—he or Hogan didn't find it when they cleared the basement out.

I should have realized it hadn't *been* there until Digger wrapped it in an old dusty rag and put it there. Dumb, dumb, dumb. Me dumb.

This analysis didn't take more than a minute, and during that minute Digger and Joe were staring at me, waiting for my reaction.

I set my coffee cup down gently. "Digger," I said, "you'd better explain where you got that gun and why you hid it in that basement. Or you'll never see another pancake in this house."

Digger grinned. "Aw, Lee. Not that!"

Joe reached over and took my hand. "No threats yet, Lee. We want to hear the whole story. First, Digger, how did you know the pistol was missing? That it had been missing—or so I think—for twenty years, since the night of the pretend holdup at the Country Convenience Store?"

"I figured it out from the story all of the guys told."

Digger fortified himself with another gulp of coffee before he went on. "Of course, before the Sharks faked the holdup on the Country Convenience Store, I kinda knew something was up. Chip and the others had been on the phone or talking out in the driveway or just generally acting as if they were planning something. They wouldn't tell me anything—I was just the kid brother. So I pretended not to even be interested."

By pretending not to listen, Digger had been able to eavesdrop and learn a few things. He hadn't understood the details of their plot, he said, except that it involved the Country Convenience Store and "guns."

"Of course, I felt sure they weren't going to shoot anybody. They kept laughing about it, you know. Not acting as if they were going to do any harm. The idea of a real robbery didn't cross my mind."

So, Digger said, he was as surprised as anybody else when he heard about the stunt and the way Brad pulled out a pistol and turned it on the rest of the Sharks. He had learned of the trick when he went down to the local teen hangout, the Corner.

But the next day Brad had called Chip, and Digger had managed to listen in.

"Brad had realized that the pistol wasn't under the counter, where he kept it," Digger said. "And Brad was afraid he was going to be in trouble with his dad over it."

"As an adult, I can see why," Joe said.

"Sure. Firing the pistol was a dumbbell thing to do. Somebody coulda been killed. So anyway, Brad told Chip that if anybody knew what had happened to that pistol, they'd better get it back to him right away. And Chip said he didn't know where it was. Brad said he was afraid to tell his dad it was gone.

"Then, a couple of days later, Brad passed the word around that the pistol had been found. His dad said he had had it. So it wasn't missing anymore. It was back in its case."

Digger frowned. "But the guys still seemed sorta worried about it. I never understood just why."

"How did the gun get into your hands?"

Digger looked sly. "I kinda found it."

"Um-hmm. Kinda found it because you knew where to look?"

"No, it was just sorta dumb luck."

"Sorta?"

Digger ducked his head and gave Joe another sly look from under his eyelids. "Sorta," he said.

Just after the holdup, Digger said, Spud backed off his friendship with the Sharks.

"I never really knew if he got mad at them, or they got mad at him. But they all just quit hanging around together."

And a couple of months later, the VHD Foundation announced its scholarship list, and Spud was right there on it. Plus, Spud quit bumming rides because he finally scraped the money together to buy a secondhand car.

"You'd think the guys would have been happy for Spud, but they weren't," Digger said. "His name was mud. And pretty soon, his name was nothing. They didn't mention Spud at all."

Digger thought the rest of the Sharks believed Spud was the last person seen with the pistol, Digger said. But they had no proof that he had taken it, hidden it, or otherwise made off with it.

"Hanged by the opinion of his peers," Joe said.

Digger drank coffee. "That's how things stood for years," he said. "Then a couple of months ago Spud called me to handle a little plumbing problem for him out at the Country Store. And the manager, Hilda, was griping to me about how she had to do everything, how Spud rarely showed up or paid any attention to the place. And she joked about his safe. Said she couldn't figure out what kind of man had such a silly thing, a little box so light anybody could walk off with it."

"So somebody did," Joe said.

Digger grinned. "I wasn't going to steal anything, Joe! In fact, I brought the box back to the store the same afternoon I took it."

"And in the meantime?"

"The lock wasn't worth piddly. I had it open in five minutes."

"And the pistol was in there?"

"Yep. I just kept it."

"Did Spud come around wanting it?"

"No. He never said a word. The way Hilda was talking, I assumed he must have forgotten all about it." Digger drank his coffee.

"I doubt he forgot it," Joe said. He kept his voice casual. "What else was in the safe? Money?"

"Nope. No money. Nothin' but a pair of shoes."

Chapter 31

Joe's head whipped toward me, and we exchanged a meaningful look.

"Can you describe the shoes?"

"They looked new," Digger said. "Not much wear, and pretty clean. Nothin' special, except it was a strange thing to find in a safe."

"What did you do with them?"

Digger grinned. "I hid them in the basement of my shop. Inside some sewer pipe. I had to put them inside it end to end. The gun was in there, too, but I decided it wasn't really a good idea to keep the gun. At all."

Digger frowned at his coffee cup. "I probably should have handed it over to the cops," he said. "But I didn't want to get involved, you know, personally. After all, I admit I stole the pistol. And the shoes. I wanted them found, but not by me.

"So when you called me about the Bailey house, I took the pistol along. I went out there early and looked at the basement door. I remembered Mrs. Bailey kept a key near that door, and sure enough, it was still there, wired to a rafter in the carport.

So I went inside and hid the pistol before Lee came. Then I went back outside and waited for her in the carport and came in the kitchen door."

He looked at Joe with trust and confidence. "So, Joe, what do I do now? Can they charge me with anything?"

"They probably could, Digger, but I doubt they will. Though you may face a lot of tough questions. I can represent you if you want me to." Joe shook his head. "Let's take a break here, and I'll try to call Hogan."

"Good," Digger said. "I need to visit your facilities anyway. Excuse me, Lee."

"Certainly, Digger. You know where those facilities are. Since you installed them."

Digger left the table and I turned to Joe.

"So that's where Curley's shoes went," I said. "Hogan was sure a tramp stole them."

"Yes, that solves one mystery. But it took me a long time to realize that Digger must have hidden the gun in the basement."

"Because it hadn't been there when you and Hogan cleared out?"

"Right. But I'm astonished that the shoes were in Spud's little safe, too. Though after Mrs. McWhirley told you and Hogan they had disappeared, I did think that Spud could have taken them. But why would he just keep them?"

"Yes, that's puzzling. I would have thought that Spud had sense enough to get rid of them. Why did he keep them hanging around?"

"I don't know. But like I told Digger, I'll call Hogan. Maybe he has some ideas."

But Joe's call to Hogan was brief. Nobody answered, either

at his house or on his cell phone. And on a Sunday, of course, no one was answering the phone at the station; on Sundays Warner Pier Police are reached through the sheriff's 9-1-1 system. Neither Joe nor I thought a 9-1-1 message was a good idea. Joe finally left a message—"Call me immediately"—on Hogan's cell phone.

By then Digger had rejoined us, and he was taking a call on his own phone. From clear across the table I could hear the excited voice of some homeowner with water all over his kitchen floor.

Digger made soothing noises and assured the client he'd be there ASAP. Then he hung up and turned to Joe.

"If you had to leave a message for Hogan, maybe I'll have time to take this call. The guy's got quite a leak."

"Probably, but leave your cell on and come back here as soon as you can, Digger. Unless you want to skip Hogan and contact the guy from the state police."

"No way! At least Hogan doesn't usually yell. This job shouldn't take long."

As soon as we saw Digger's truck heading down the road, I gave a deep sigh. "I think Aunt Nettie and Hogan were going to church today. The granddaughter of her pal Hazel was going to sing. Personally, I'm glad to have a little time to think over the significance of what Digger told us."

"I think we can now take a guess at who was in the men's room during the so-called holdup."

"Curley McWhirley."

Joe nodded. "That seems pretty logical. For one thing, everybody in the neighborhood knew that Curley had been in the habit of walking to the convenience store every evening."

"To buy a Hershey bar."

"Right. Since he walked, his car wouldn't be in the parking lot. That fooled the Sharks. They thought the store was empty of customers, but Curley was still inside."

"And Curley's reaction to hearing somebody yell, 'This is a holdup!' must have been like mine would have been."

Joe laughed. "Jump in the restroom and lock the door?"

"Exactly. And that was twenty years ago. People didn't carry cell phones much then. But Sharpy said that Brad checked the men's room and said he found no one there."

"Curley probably just didn't want to come out. He would have been embarrassed and wouldn't have wanted the Sharks to know he was there."

"If Curley had had any sense of humor," I said, "he could have had a great story."

"True. But I never heard of Curley having a sense of humor."

"Neither did I. So we can assume Curley wouldn't have been amused by being caught up in a teenage prank."

Joe nodded. "And that may explain why Brad didn't want the rest of the Sharks to help him clean up. He was helping Curley hide, then trying to calm him down."

"Joe!" I clutched his arm. "Joe! That explains the shoes. I mean, it could explain why Spud bothered to hide them all these years! Curley must have stepped in the Frozen Rainbow!"

Joe chuckled. "I think you've got it. I'll bet the shoes prove Curley was in the Country Store when that stupid prank went down! If no one's worn them, they might even still have sugary residue on them."

"But Joe," I said, "there are a lot of questions unanswered. Such as where does Vic VanHorn fit in? He must be part of it. Or could we just have a mad shooter around here?"

"I might have an idea on that. But it's pretty far-fetched."

I groaned. "I think I have an idea, too. And it's almost un-believable."

We stared at each other a moment. Then Joe spoke. "Right. But let's shelve that a moment and think about the situation. The Sharks come to the Country Store to pull a fake holdup on Brad. Brad surprises them by having a gun."

"And firing it into the Frozen Rainbow tank."

"True. This causes Curley to hide in the restroom.

"The Sharks offer to clean up the spilled Frozen Rainbow, but Brad says he doesn't need help and sends them away. Then he lets Curley out of the men's room. Now, how would Curley feel after this experience?"

"Hmm," I said. "From what we know of him, I'd say he'd be mad as the dickens. I know his widow loved him, but most people thought he was a stuffy old crank. I'd expect him to come out of the men's room furious."

"Brad was probably afraid he'd have another heart attack."

I gasped. "Oh gosh, Joe! And Curley did have one!"

"I think a heart attack would be unlikely. Apparently he had returned to work, and the doctors had given him a clean bill of health."

"But, Joe, he did have a heart attack! He left the Country Store on foot, and he walked home. About a mile. Then he col-lapsed by the side of the road, in his own driveway. That's where Dr. Davis found him, dead from a heart attack!"

We both thought that over for a minute or so. Then Joe spoke. "Lee, why was Dr. Davis there?"

"Supposedly, he saw that there was an emergency and sim-ply pulled over."

We thought some more.

Then Joe spoke. "I think Brad must have called his dad and told him what happened."

His remark was like the sun rising. "Of course," I said. "Brad was just a kid. Here he was in a lonely store. His friends had pulled a mean trick on him. Then he finds out a prominent local crank was a witness to the whole stunt. And the local crank is breathing fire and threatening to call the cops. Or somebody. How would you feel?"

"I'd have been terrified," Joe said. "I'd have called home—looking for adult support." He leaned forward and shook his finger at me. "That explains why Dr. Davis was there."

"What do you mean?"

"He didn't just happen by. Brad called his dad and he went to talk to Curley. Either Dr. Davis would use his status as a VanHorn-Davis to intimidate Curley—"

"Which doesn't sound as if it would work."

"No, it doesn't. Frankly, it sounds more like Curley would try harder to threaten trouble for Dr. Davis or for Brad."

"The whole thing gives me a picture of two middle-aged men standing beside the road yelling at each other."

"While Brad was back at the Country Store, mopping up Frozen Rainbow."

We stopped to think again.

"Our speculations leave Spud, the gun, and the disappearing shoes out completely. Not to mention Vic VanHorn," I said.

Joe frowned. "But they add Dr. Davis to the mix," he said.

I considered that. "I think you're right," I said. "Dr. Davis would have tracked down Curley and tried to convince him that the holdup was just a teenage prank and that he should let it go. Maybe he lost his temper. Maybe Curley didn't die of a heart attack after all!"

"So Dr. Davis killed him? That's pretty extreme and, after twenty years, would be really hard to prove."

We stared at each other glumly. Finally I stood up. "I guess I'll do the dishes, change clothes, and put on some makeup."

"Where are you going?"

"If you and Digger are going to talk to Hogan and bring up Dr. Davis, I might want to go along."

Joe rolled his eyes. "The girl who never wants to miss anything."

I grabbed the coffee carafe from the table as I headed for the kitchen sink. But as I reached the back door, I changed my plans.

Dr. Drew Davis was standing there, staring at me.

Chapter 32

I've had surprises in my life, but that one was a real humdinger. Joe and I had been saying that doctors don't simply happen by. Yet here one was. And it was a doctor I didn't particularly want to see at that moment.

Could he have heard Joe and me talking? All our doors and windows were open. Had he overheard our speculation about his connection to the death of Curley McWhirley? The thought paralyzed me.

He spoke. "Hello, Mrs. Woodyard."

"Good morning, Dr. Davis. I didn't hear you."

"I wanted to speak to your husband."

"Certainly." I squawked, "Joe!" And my squawk made me realize I was scared to death.

"Joe!" I squawked again. Then I pushed the screen door open, and I forced my voice to be calm and quiet. "Please come in."

I might have been scared, but I had to act as if this were a normal call and that Dr. Davis was a normal caller. I fixed my mind on that goal, and I led the doctor through the kitchen and the dining room. I didn't stop until we reached the living room. Then I invited him to sit down. He didn't sit.

I even waved the carafe I was holding. "Coffee?"

"No, thank you," he said. "I just wanted to ask your husband a few questions."

There was no sign of Joe in the living room, so I decided that he must have gone into the bedroom. *Should I call him out, squawking again? Or should I hope he realized that something's wrong and has taken shelter somewhere else in the house?* There was no reason for both of us to die in this encounter with Dr. Davis.

What a dumb idea, I told myself. No one was going to die. The doctor was acting like a perfect gentleman. I was the one who was lacking poise. And I wasn't going to kill anybody.

"I'll try to find Joe," I said. "I guess he's dressing."

I went into the bedroom from the living room. I was closing the door behind me when I realized that Dr. Davis was with me, accompanying me on a trip to haul my husband out of the bathroom.

That wasn't polite. In fact, it was downright rude.

I stopped and turned to face Dr. Davis. I tried to make my words sound just slightly miffed. "I'll find Joe and bring him out, Dr. Davis. You can wait in the living room."

We stood eye to eye. Neither of us moved. Then I squawked again. "Joe! Joe!"

Davis put his hand over my mouth, and he grabbed my arm with his other hand. "Please be quiet," he said. "We'll wait here until your husband comes."

Almost immediately the door to the back hall opened, and

Joe stood in the opening. "What's the matter?" he said. "Can't a guy shave?"

Then he saw what was going on.

For a moment the three of us stood immobile. Then Dr. Davis clutched his fist over my mouth more tightly. He spun me around, still with his hand over my mouth, and pulled me against his chest.

And I realized that a pistol was against my temple.

"Let her go," Joe said. "I'll do anything you want. But let Lee go."

"I'm sorry," Dr. Davis said. "I'm afraid you both must obey me."

"Dr. Davis," Joe said, "let's discuss this logically."

"It's too late for that, Mr. Woodyard. You and your wife should close your windows before you discuss sensitive matters."

"But . . ." Joe spoke again, but I had the feeling he didn't really have a good idea about what to say.

And at that moment a very unwelcome sound entered the mix.

"Joe! Lee!" It was Digger. He banged on the back door. Then he yelled.

"It's Digger! I'm back! That guy found the cutoff! The call was canceled!"

For a brief moment my heart jumped with hope. Then it sank. I realized in dismay that all our bedroom curtains were closed. Joe and I were confronting a criminal in the one room in our house that no one could see into.

Digger banged on the door again. Then he yelled again. Bang. Yell. Bang. Yell.

Dr. Davis, Joe, and I all stood immobile. Or almost immobile. Dr. Davis's lips did move. Using the pistol for emphasis, he mouthed one word.

"Quiet."

We obeyed. And after a few minutes that seemed like an hour, Digger went away. He muttered and swore, but he did nothing more. His footsteps gradually faded. We heard his truck start. His tires crunched down the drive.

Digger was gone. The only person likely to drop by and help us had left, never realizing how much we needed that help.

Dr. Davis gave a sigh. "Now, Mrs. Woodyard, I'll let go of you. You move over by your husband and take his hand. Both of you continue to face me. Holding hands."

I obeyed, turning around and moving to Joe's side. He took my hand and squeezed it tightly. I squeezed back.

Dr. Davis sighed again. "I think we need one more thing, Mr. Woodyard. The keys to the house across the way. As I walked into this room, I saw a bunch of keys on the dresser. Is the key to that house among them?"

Joe nodded. "It has a cardboard tag."

"Ah, good." Davis backed up.

I could feel Joe's muscles tense. After all, he had been a state champion wrestler. If Davis was even slightly distracted, I knew Joe would jump him. And I hoped he would tear him limb from limb.

I let the hand Joe was holding go limp. If he needed to move quickly, I didn't want to slow him down.

But Dr. Davis didn't have even a moment of distraction. He walked backward toward the dresser, and when he reached it, he felt around its top and picked out the key with the cardboard tag. Lifting it in front of his eyes, he read the label.

"Ah," he said. "'Bailey house.' I think that would be a much safer place for us to confer."

"Why?" I couldn't help asking.

"Privacy. That idiot plumber is likely to come back. So let's head to the door to the living room. And as you pass the dresser, Mrs. Woodyard, you may place that carafe on it."

I had completely forgotten I was holding that darn carafe. I stared at it. Could I throw it at him? Could I pour coffee down his back?

But Joe was shaking his head. And I knew he was right. If I tried to lift my arm, Davis could fire before I could get the carafe in tossing position. And he was moving away from me. I wasn't going to be close enough to pour the hot coffee on him.

So the three of us went into the living room in a carefully contrived arrangement of captives and captor. And, yes, I remembered to put the carafe on the dresser.

"Just go out the front door," Dr. Davis said. "We'll walk down the driveway to the Bailey place."

And that's what we did. Joe and I, each afraid of causing injury to the other, led the way to the Bailey house. Dr. Davis followed. An elaborate series of movements allowed him to open the front door. We went inside, still edging gingerly around, and we somehow got down the basement stairs. Joe and I ended up standing on the sandy floor, with Dr. Davis facing us. His back was to the door that led to the outside.

And never, never, did Dr. Davis let the hand holding the gun drop down or lose its aim toward the two of us.

After everything was arranged to suit him, he spoke.

"And now," he said, "I need to know where those shoes are."

Shoes? For a moment I was baffled. Of course I remembered them almost immediately, but why did Dr. Davis want them?

Joe put on his professional voice and said, "We don't have the shoes, and I recommend that you tell your story to the authorities. I'm sure McWhirley's death was merely an accident."

"I can't do that, Mr. Woodyard. No, I'm committed to this plan of action. And it means I need the shoes."

"I told you we don't have the shoes," Joe said. "We don't even know where they are."

I couldn't stay silent. "If you listened to us talk our ideas out, you know that we didn't say anything about where the shoes are."

"And 'ideas' is the right word," Joe said. "We were simply tossing out ideas about what might have happened. We have no proof of anything."

He lowered his voice and spoke in a confidential manner. "Even if everything we said were true, Dr. Davis, we have nothing to substantiate our speculations. As a lawyer, I'd advise you to simply ignore such talk."

Davis sighed deeply. "The problem with that, Mr. Woodyard, is that gossip is the enemy of professional men. I don't have to be convicted to be ruined. That 'talk' you mentioned could do it. I need those shoes. Now!"

Joe spoke again. "We're at an impasse," he said.

Or I think that's what he said. Actually I was too distracted to be sure. Something was happening behind Dr. Davis, and I couldn't tell just what it was.

I was getting only glimpses through the ground-level windows behind the doctor. Something was moving out there.

Something? Or was it someone? Was that a shoe, walking past? Was it the leg of some blue jeans? Who could be there? Was it all my imagination?

Meanwhile, Joe was still talking, talking in a soothing voice, the one he used when he wanted to wear a witness down until an incriminating answer was blurted out.

And I was becoming more and more terrified. Who was outside? Was it a friend? Or was it another foe?

Joe's calmness wasn't working on Dr. Davis. The man was getting angrier and angrier. Joe moved slightly in front of me—a heroic gesture, but one that was even more frightening. Then the doctor raised his pistol.

"I can't take this!" he said. "If you can't tell me, I'll just have to end the situation!"

He pulled the hammer of the pistol back.

And an ungodly noise broke loose.

Somebody yelled like a banshee, then howled like a wolf. Two heavy pieces of metal clanged in unearthly rhythms. I screamed.

Joe threw my hand down and rushed the doctor. A pistol shot echoed off the walls of the basement. The old high school wrestler grabbed his opponent in a headlock. The pistol flew across the room. I rushed after it and picked it up.

Joe and Dr. Davis fell in a heap of arms and legs in the middle of the floor, and the outside door to the basement flew open.

It was Digger. He ran to me, and his lips moved.

Of course, thanks to the gunshot, I couldn't hear a thing he said. I just pointed at Joe, wrestling with Dr. Davis as if he were still sixteen.

"Help Joe! Help Joe!" I doubt Digger could hear anything either.

It was several minutes before my ears began to work. And the first thing I heard was a siren.

It sounded beautiful.

Chapter 33

We were saved by a combination of circumstances. Providence? Good fortune? Dumb luck? Or simply Digger?

Of course it was late that afternoon before we figured all that out. It took explanations from Digger, from us, from Brad, and from Hogan to understand it all.

As Digger had left our house, pulling onto Lake Shore Drive to take his emergency service call, he saw a black car coming toward him and recognized it as belonging to Dr. Davis. Looking into his rearview mirror, he realized it was turning into our lane.

He drove on, but after the recent conversation, Dr. Davis's presence at our house bothered him. After half a mile, he swung into a driveway, turned around, and went back.

"I tried to sneak into your place," Digger said. "I felt stupid to be so suspicious, but when I found Dr. Davis's car parked on that back drive that leads out to the other road—well, it just made me awful nervous. So I parked in your driveway and went to the back door."

We heard Digger yelling and banging on the kitchen door,

but Joe and I couldn't answer because Dr. Davis was holding us at gunpoint. So Digger went away. But he didn't go far. He called 9-1-1 and talked to the emergency operator, even though he wasn't sure anything was wrong.

"I thought I'd rather look like a fool than actually be one," he said.

Next Digger armed himself with two heavy wrenches from the back of his truck. By then Dr. Davis was marching Joe and me across to the Bailey house. Digger caught sight of us and followed, jumping behind bushes so he wouldn't be seen.

After we all reached the Bailey house, Digger found the Baileys' extra key, still on the carport rafter. He unlocked the outside door to the basement, then knelt beside a window to keep an eye on what was happening.

"When I saw the doctor aiming that pistol at you two," he said, "I began to make loud noises with those wrenches and some metal I found back there. And I hollered." Digger smiled happily. "I knew that Joe would take care of things if I could just get the doctor distracted."

Joe shook his head. "I wish I had felt that confident, Digger. It's been a long time since I was a wrestler. I was sure every minute that Dr. Davis was going to shoot us both."

"I wish something else," I said. "I wish I knew where Vic VanHorn fit into this whole deal."

"Oh, that one's easy," Hogan said. "He'd been involved since the night Dr. Drew Davis shot Curley McWhirley."

"Did the doctor really do that?" I asked.

"We haven't got the full story yet," Hogan said. "Brad explained most of that—after his father was arrested. Brad had never understood everything he knew about McWhirley's death. Now he's cooperating fully.

"After the so-called holdup, Spud forgot his hoodie at the Country Convenience Store. When he went back to get it, he must have overheard Brad telling his dad that Curley had been present for the holdup and that he had gone away breathing threats at all the Sharks. Dr. Davis assured Brad he would take care of the situation and went off to do that, taking the pistol with him.

"Spud—always nosy," Hogan said, "followed along and reached the spot where Curley was found just as the two men were having a big argument. The pistol went off; Curley fell dead.

"It could have been an accident," Hogan said. "It could have been manslaughter. It could have been murder.

"From a hiding place in the trees, Spud continued to listen. Vic VanHorn arrived in his hearse. Spud heard Dr. Davis trying to convince Vic that he should help hide the cause of Curley's death."

"No autopsy, then," I said.

Hogan shook his head. "It wasn't needed, since McWhirley's own doctor—Dr. Drew Davis—was there to certify the cause of death. Vic signed off on the papers, loaded McWhirley into the hearse, allowed Mrs. McWhirley a look at her husband, and took him away to the mortuary."

"I guess there's no way to prove anything now," I said.

Hogan nodded. "Hiding a fatal shooting would require the cooperation of both the shooter and the funeral director who handled the body. Of course Dr. Davis was in a position to bring this about."

"It's surprising that Vic would go along with the plan," Joe said.

"Twenty years ago," Hogan said, "Vic was new in town and trying to make a business go. He would certainly have wanted to get along with everybody, maybe especially the doctor in town. When Davis called him to pick up a body, he would have probably accepted the doctor's word that the shooting was an accident."

I was still having trouble picturing Dr. Davis as a killer. "I thought something funny had gone on, but I never thought about the doctor actually killing Curley."

"That's the most logical explanation," Hogan said. "And Vic agreed to help him cover up the crime. But the load on Vic's conscience, or so he says, finally got so heavy he told Dr. Davis he was going to confess. That's when Vic called Joe, wanting Joe to help him find a good lawyer. But Vic and Davis argued, and Davis ended up shooting Vic's car full of holes, and shooting Vic at the same time."

"How badly is Vic injured?" I asked.

"He'll live," Hogan said. "We've got him hidden in a hospital—not one in Holland. He wanted to have an attorney before he would talk to us. That happened this afternoon."

"Maybe," Joe said, "the original shooting actually was an accident."

"Could be," Hogan said. "But it won't matter. Hitting Spud in the head with a two-by-four is murder no matter how you look at it. That's a more likely charge."

I shook my head. "So Dr. Davis killed Spud, too. Why?"

"To hide the fact that Spud had been blackmailing him," Hogan said. "Spud wound up stealing both the pistol and Mc-

Whirley's walking shoes, or so we believe, by taking them from
Dr. Davis's car. We think Dr. Davis took the shoes off McWhirley's feet to hide the fact that they had Frozen Rainbow on
them. And Dr. Davis had probably left the pistol in the car, too.
So all Spud had to do was reach in and take them."

"And both the shoes and the pistol were linked to McWhirley's death by forensic evidence," Joe said.

"Right," Hogan said. "Spud was blackmailing Dr. Davis,
but apparently he managed to keep the doctor from knowing
who was doing it."

I frowned. "It's hard to believe Dr. Davis hadn't figured out
who was asking him for money."

"Apparently Spud asked for small amounts of money at a
time. Dr. Davis must have figured it was safer to pay than to
try to eliminate the blackmailer, a person whose identity was
unknown to him. But when Spud tried to get a larger sum
of money—enough to develop the orchard and the Bailey
house, plus another tract he had plans for—well, he must have
tipped his hand. Davis was able to figure out who the blackmailer was."

"Dr. Davis finally understood who was milking him?"

"That's my guess," Hogan said. "Dr. Davis followed Spud
until he isolated him at the Bailey place, then used a two-by-
four to kill him."

Joe frowned. "How did ownership of the Country Convenience Store get mixed up in the blackmail?"

"According to Brad," Hogan said, "several years after the
phony holdup, Dr. Davis decided to sell the place. By then Spud
was working in real estate, so he would have learned that it was

for sale. We haven't traced just how he worked the deal, but Spud wound up owning the store. It may have been a legitimate purchase, using the money he'd gained through blackmail. Later he sold the store to that management company."

"At least Edna McWhirley will now know what happened to the missing shoes," I said. "And she'll understand what actually happened to her husband! But, what about the money stashed at the Country Convenience Store?"

"I think that was an emergency fund Spud left there, or part of it. And a hiding place for the shoes. But remember, Digger took the pistol and the shoes. But he didn't find any cash at the store. Spud hid the money there later."

Joe was still frowning. "The 'Tater' notes will always mystify me," he said. "Hogan, where was the first one found?"

"In the pocket of the jacket Spud was wearing when he was killed. I think it was put there as an attempt to link you to the murder. Brad admits his dad pumped him about the nicknames. And apparently Davis heard enough about the Sharks' business to mistakenly think that you were a member. He missed the part where you turned down their invitation."

"And Dr. Davis borrowed Vic's car the night of the attack on Jerry Cherry," Hogan said. "The cars look similar. At least, they do in the dark. Both small and black."

We all stared at one another, shaking our heads.

"A weird case," Hogan said. "A lot of mistakes and misunderstandings."

Gradually the Warner Pier community came to understand what had happened. The people I've felt sorry for, of course, are Brad and Felicia Davis. Not many events can cause a real community scandal these days, but Dr. Davis's behavior certainly did it.

A few weeks later Felicia called us and asked if she and Brad could come out to talk. Naturally, we said yes. Equally naturally, we didn't really want them to come.

But I made coffee and prepared an assortment of Christmas goodies—small chocolate Santa Claus figures, cranberry orange cinnamon truffles, mint bonbons, and eggnog truffles.

But I loaded the serving dishes with dread in my soul. Were Brad and Felicia going to ask some special favor for Dr. Davis?

But they didn't. Both simply asked us to forgive Brad's father, if we could. His lawyers were saying it seemed very unlikely that he'd ever be released from prison.

And they said they hoped that the four of us could continue our friendship.

We assured them we could certainly try to keep that friendship alive.

"We thought of moving away," Brad said. "But there seemed little point in that. In today's world there are no secrets. Our friends and families are going to know what happened. I remember that—well, I think I suspected my dad was mixed up in something funny the night of the fake holdup. When he wasn't charged or even investigated, I got frightened, and the episode left a distance between the two of us for—what?—all these years. Oddly, after all this commotion, we're finally able to talk normally again."

Brad smiled. "Heck! This is the age of Google! Even if we move, other people will be able to find us. Felicia and I think we'll be able to live with the situation here in Warner Pier as well as anywhere else."

"Good," I said. "Maggie's been terrified that she'd have to find a new board member for the Showboat project."

Felicia held her chin high. "Oh, I'm still planning to be on board the Showboat," she said. "Break a leg!"

Oatmeal Chocolate Drop Cookies

The family was gathering for Thanksgiving, and my menu assignment was cookies. Any kind. Just cookies.

I naturally made the easiest ones I know how to make.

As I walked into the host kitchen, my daughter greeted me. "Here are the cookies," I said.

"Put them on the counter," she said. "I'm trying not to eat anything sweet this year."

I followed instructions, placing the tin box of cookies in an out-of-the-way corner, and taking the cover off.

"Oh!" my daughter said. "You brought *that* kind!" She snatched up a couple and wolfed them down.

Oatmeal chocolate drops may destroy your diet plans, but they sure are good.

¼ cup cocoa

2 cups sugar

½ cup milk

1 stick margarine

½ cup peanut butter

1 teaspoon vanilla

3 cups raw oatmeal

Mix cocoa, sugar, and milk in large saucepan. Add margarine, bring to a boil, and cook for one minute. Stir in peanut butter, vanilla, and oatmeal. Drop teaspoons of mixture onto waxed paper. Let stand until room temperature. Enjoy!

NOV -- 2019.